HELLO DARKNESS

HELLO DARKNESS

ANTHONY McGOWAN

WALKER
BOOKS

First published 2013 by Walker Books Ltd
87 Vauxhall Walk, London SE11 5HJ

2 4 6 8 10 9 7 5 3

Text © 2013 Anthony McGowan
Cover design © 2013 Walker Books Ltd

This book has been typeset in Slimbach

Printed and bound in Great Britain by Clays Ltd, St Ives plc

British Library Cataloguing in Publication Data:
a catalogue record for this book is available from the British Library

ISBN 978-1-4063-3784-6

www.walker.co.uk

For Rebecca Campbell, whose silken thread guided me through the labyrinth

DAY ONE
Tuesday

CHAPTER ONE
You Oscillate It

I was sitting on the can when it all kicked off. Third cubicle from the wall. You could be pretty sure of finding me there at 11.30 on a Tuesday morning. That's because 11.30 on a Tuesday morning meant double maths, and even the sour tang in the boys' *pissoir* beat the heck out of quadratic equations, and the stale pleasure of speculating about whether Mr McHale would be wearing the brown safari jacket with red food stains, or the red jacket with brown stains.

I'd grown kind of fond of cubicle number three. The busted lock meant it was never used for any of the more depressing activities that can happen in school toilet cubicles, and the graffiti in there was of a slightly higher standard than usual, including the classic:

How do you titillate an ocelot?

I could usually while away an hour pondering such matters, but this morning I had other things on my mind. My great aunt or some such obscure relation had shuffled off her mortal coil, and Dad, Mum and Sis were going to throw dirt on the coffin. This was all happening down on the coast and they were set to be away for the week. It was my first time alone in the house, which was cool. But Mum and Dad kept hammering me about my meds, even as they were lined up by the door, all ready to go.

"You'll take your pills, John?"

"Sure, Mum."

"The white, red and blue ones?"

"I know, Mum. The white, red and the blue."

"You understand why?"

"I'm not an idiot…"

"The boy'll be fine," said Dad, and gave me a look that was supposed to say *I trust you*, but had too much raw hope in it for that. "Come on, we've got to get going."

I picked up my sis, and held her high and shook her till she giggled.

"Bye, John-John," she said, and I lowered her down so she could kiss my cheek.

On the way out of the house I looked at the special

dispenser with thirty-one compartments, containing my medication for every day of the month. A white, a red and a blue in each little box. But I was late and in a mad rush and I told myself that it would be OK if I took them when I got back from school.

So I was playing the goodbye scene over again in my head in cubicle three when I heard the door to the toilets creak open, and felt that electric line of tension crawl across my shoulders.

There were a couple of possibilities. It could be some kid who'd put up his hand in class and begged to be allowed to relieve himself. The alternative was that it was one of the Shank's patrols.

This was a more troubling prospect.

The Shank – or Mr Shankley to give him his full name – was the new Deputy, brought in to "save our failing school", although that turned out to be pretty much in the way the harpoon saves the whale. There was no escaping Shankley. He was all over us like scabs on a leper. A crew-cut Nosferatu, he prowled the corridors looking for kids to murder. His preferred weapon was a voice that could either slit you open with the sly precision of a stiletto, or blow your head off like a roadside bomb.

So, you can see why I wasn't too pleased to hear the toilet door creak open.

I pulled my legs up and hoped the Shank – if it was him – would settle for a quick look under the row of cubicles. Of course, if he went to each stall and kicked back the door, then I'd be up to my neck in the brown stuff.

What happened was a pause, a rustle, then a sort of faint skittering noise, like the sound of peanut shells falling out of a bag. Then there was a metallic rattle, loud enough to make me jump. And then, well, then some other sound that might have been a cough, or a laugh, or just one of those untranslatable noises that bodies make sometimes.

Then the door opened and closed, and I was on my own again.

All kinds of intriguing. So, up I got and pulled open the cubicle door, using the upperside of my foot on the lowerside of the door, because, frankly, you don't want to be touching *anything* in there with your hands.

I wasn't expecting much, and not much is what I found.

At first.

In fact, not much seemed to be selling it big, because what it looked like was nothing at all. The room was empty. The six sinks still stood in a line, echoed by the six yellowing urinals on the opposite wall. With the six cubicles, that made 666, the number of the beast. Some architect's idea of a joke? Or maybe Satan himself liked to hang out here, skiving off from maths lessons in hell.

Then I looked down at the floor tiles. Once white, but a lot of amber liquid had flowed this way over the years. There was something on the floor – besides the archaeological deposits of urine, that is.

No, some *things* on the floor.

Dry, brown things.

My eyes didn't want to focus. I moved closer and bent to study the *whatever-they-were* scattered across the tiles. I stretched out my fingers, not meaning to touch them, but just assessing the scale of them, getting their dimensions into my head.

Then a couple of things happened pretty close together, and I really couldn't say which was first. One was the door opening again, and one was me realizing that these dry, brown things had once lived in a glass tank in the biology lab. I think that my lips may even have begun forming the words "stick insects", when I looked up into four cruel eyes and two malicious smiles.

CHAPTER TWO
SOCKED

AS I looked up, Bosola and Funt looked down.

This was *not* good.

Shankley himself would have been grim, but at least you'd know roughly what to expect. You'd get yelled at, and you'd get detention. You might get suspended. You might get expelled. But you wouldn't get your head kicked in. With these two jokers you couldn't rely on that.

Bosola and Funt weren't the kind of kids you'd normally expect to find wearing prefects' badges, but then that went for all the prefects in our school. The Shank had hand-picked the scumbags, and trained them up to act as his bullyboys and enforcers, thereby neatly getting round the quaint rule that said the teachers weren't permitted to kick seven types of *merde* out of you any more. The prefects had a thumb in almost every racket that went on in the school, from bun-running for the Lardies to the tax on the Year Seven's dinner money, extracted in a very business-like manner at the school gates. They also ran the lucrative trade in stolen exam papers, and the word was that the Shank got a ten per cent kickback for turning a blind eye.

These two badasses were the lowest of the low. Funt was the muscle and he followed Bosola around the way a foul burp follows a cheap burger. Funt looked like one of those Easter Island statues, and his conversation was just as lively. He was an idiot savant – you know, one of those guys who can't tie his shoelaces or catch a bus, but have one special ability, like knowing pi to a million decimal places, or being able to remember exact cloud formations on a particular day when he was six years old. Funt's special ability was that he could punch you in the mouth and spit in your eye at the same time.

OK, so maybe not such a savant. Maybe just an idiot idiot. An idiot squared. Either way, he was the nearest the duo got to a good cop.

Bad-cop Bosola looked like a girl, but if ever you bumped into him it was a good idea to check afterwards to make sure your throat hadn't gotten itself accidentally slit. He was a pink-eyed, white-haired albino, but he died his hair black and wore coloured contact lenses. It was said that if he took his contacts out and gave you his pink-eyed stare, you'd go mad or drop down dead or, at the very least, soil yourself – but I reckoned that was just his PR machine, and deep down he was a sissy. He spoke with the sinister high-pitched whine of a dentist's drill:

"Oh, now just when I thought the day was a write-off, here it is, like a gift from heaven, wacko Middleton, squirming like a cockroach on the toilet floor."

Funt grunted. It was the sound you'd get from a pig when you put its slops out at feeding time.

"And what do we do to a crap-house roach?" continued Bosola's whine.

"We stamp on it," replied Funt, his voice rumbling like a dumper truck in a quarry. And he stepped forward, ready to put precisely that plan into operation.

But before the stamp, came a crunch.

"What the…?" said Funt, looking down. He lifted up his shoe and peered at the sole, like a caveman trying to work out how to change the fuse on a plug.

Bosola checked out the floor too. He also looked puzzled. Then he smiled. "This is nice. This is better than nice. We haven't just got some skiver; we've got a psycho."

"Wait a minute," I said, getting up. "I found these here, same as you."

"Not what it looks like to me, pal," said Bosola. "Mr Shankley's gonna do his nut when he sees this. He loves his little pets, doesn't he, Futs?"

Another grunt from the monolith. He peeled a stick insect off his shoe, like spiky gum.

Bosola was right about one thing. As part of the New Regime, Shankley had filled the school with all kinds of animals. The thinking was that it would diffuse some of the violence, bring in a dash of that "*awwww*, ain't it cute" vibe. So that's why we had those damn stick insects in the biology lab, as well as three nervous (and eggless) chickens in a run near the playing fields, a couple of guinea pigs called Snuffy and Sniffy in the Sixth Form common room and, most important of all, a tortoise called the Venerable Bede, who was the official school mascot.

Actually, the tortoise wasn't part of the New Deal. He'd always belonged to our Principal, Mr Vole, and was said to be the same age as the old man.

The Shank used the poor beasts in his Friday assembly orations, lauding the loyalty of the guinea pigs, the sagacity of the tortoise, and the community spirit of the chickens, who would happily have given up their eggs if they'd ever managed to lay any. Maybe, for all I can remember, he even praised the artful cunning of the stick insects.

But now the stick insects had gone for the big sleep and I was up to my neck in manure.

"Pick 'em up," said Bosola, looking me in the eye.

"Pick 'em up yourself," I said amiably back, though amiable is not quite the right word for the thoughts in my head. I knew that the second I bent to pick up the insects, I'd get a boot in the face. "If you don't mind standing aside, I've got to get back to class – I've a hot date with a really sexy quadratic equation."

Suddenly Bosola's soft, feminine face hardened.

"Oh, so he doesn't want to pick 'em up! Doesn't he know that we're prefects, and that as he's just a Year-Ten zero, he's got to do what we say?"

Funt grunted.

I still didn't move.

"So, in that case it's back to plan A," said Bosola.

Funt looked at him uncertainly.

Bosola gave a little groan. "The stamping!"

"Oh, yeah."

Now, Funt was slow, but only in the sense of being thick. When it came to using his body rather than his mind, he was anything but sluggish. He reached me in two quick, boxer's steps. I put my left up to parry his right, but it didn't come. Instead he grabbed my throat and shoved me back against the wall, keeping a hold on my neck. Now he drew back his fist, going for a straight right to the middle of my face. It's the sort of punch you use on little kids. A nose buster or lip burster. It won't put down a real fighter – you need a nice clean hit to the chin to do that – but it'll make a kid cry.

The trouble was, I now didn't have the time to parry, or even duck, not with Funt's speed of hand. So I rolled my face to the right, and the punch slid off the side of my skull, like a rock bouncing down a mountain, and smashed into the wall behind me.

Funt yowled and let go of my neck. He was still in close, so I gave him a back-handed slap with my left to make some room. The slap made a good noise as my knuckles rapped against his hard bones. I stepped out from his shadow and drew back my arm, going for the thinnest part of the jaw. I gave myself a 50–50 chance of cracking it.

But halfway there, my fist sort of died. It took me a second to realize that I'd been sapped. I found that I was down on my knees. I looked up. Bosola was holding something. Something soft with something hard inside it. Then he swung it again and the world went supernova.

CHAPTER THREE
The Shank

"WHAT d'ya sock him with?"

"A sock."

"A sock?"

"A sock with a spud in it."

"How d'ya find a sock with a spud in it?"

"I put the spud in the sock."

"Oh. Why d'ya put the spud in the sock?"

"Jeez. Look, a spud in a sock makes a good cosh. It takes a guy down. But if you get pulled in, what have you got? Just a sock and a spud. You put the sock on, you eat the spud. Right?"

"Right."

Well, that was the quality of entertainment I had on the trip, once I came round. The two of them were half dragging, half carrying me along. One of them had hold of my shirt collar, choking the air out of me. I think that's what brought me round, dying being one of the things I'll gladly wake up to avoid. I tried to get my feet to take some of the weight, but they slipped and slid on the polished floor of the corridor.

"Looks like the baby woke up."

They held me low and hard, so I had to trot along bent double. We went up a flight of stairs, along another corridor. Twice I stumbled, and twice they hauled me up by the collar, each time yanking it tighter.

And then we were outside the Shank's office.

I should give you some geography. And maybe a bit of history. We were in the section of the school called the teachers' corridor. You'd know it with your eyes closed: it was the only part of the school that didn't smell of disinfectant and urine. First, you came to the school office, where the secretary, a spinster called Miss Bickersniff lived, then the staff room, then the Shank's office with a sign saying Chief Executive on the door, and then the Principal's office.

The Principal, Mr Vole, was a sweet old guy, smelling faintly of pipe smoke and peppermint, with a whiff of fruitcake. His milky eyes peered benignly over the top of a pair of half-moon glasses, and his only desire, so far as anyone could tell, was to get through to his retirement with as little bother as possible.

Before the Shank came along, most of the work fell on the shoulders of the old Deputy, a fuzzy-haired guy called Mr Bathgate. Bathgate was a nervous breakdown waiting to happen, and after yet another disastrous school inspection he had a total collapse. Miss Bickersniff found him sitting on the wastepaper bin in his office, with his pants shucked down around his ankles, shouting for his mummy.

So, Shankley was brought in as the new broom, and everything changed. The old sweet chaos was replaced by fastened top buttons and lots of shouting. The thinking behind it all was to run the place like a business, which was why Shankley had that Chief Executive nameplate put up on his door. Much to his obvious bemusement, Vole found himself described as the "Managing Director". But the truth was, the school was now more like a military dictatorship than either a corporation or an institution of learning.

Bosola knocked on Shankley's door. A bark came from inside. Then the door was open, and I was facing the Shank across a wooden desk as big as an aircraft carrier.

Facing Mr Shankley wasn't something you'd

choose to do for entertainment. His eyes were a weird pale-green – so pale, in fact, that sometimes it seemed that there was no line between the white of the eye and the iris. He wore his sparse, gun-metal-grey hair slicked back, and his mouth was twisted into a near-perpetual snarl, which only occasionally softened itself into a sneer. If he could have got away with it, he'd have gone full-on Gestapo and added a monocle and leather gloves.

The Shank's narrow lips pursed. He had a wart like a rice crispy on the side of his nose.

"What is this?"

"Sir, we found this slimeball in the bogs. I mean toilets, sir. And not just that, sir, but he had *these*."

Bosola elbowed Funt.

Funt reached into his pocket and took out a dirty handkerchief. He shook it over the Shank's desk. A dozen dead bodies fell out, rattling on the polished wood.

The Shank started back from his desk. His face went blank for a moment, and then weirdly tight, as if it had been suddenly shrink-wrapped.

Then he said, in a voice hardly more than a whisper, "Explain."

I wanted to get my story in first. "I was—" I began, but the Shank cut me off.

"NOT YOU!" he yelled, his voice now scalpel-sharp. "And sort that collar and tie out!"

I thought about a sardonic remark on the subject of who had messed up my collar and tie, but this wasn't a good time for sardonic remarks.

"Like I said, sir, we found him skiving in the toilets. These things were on the floor, scattered all around him. It looked like he'd just chucked them there the second before we came in."

The Shank turned his pale eyes on me again, and I'd be a liar if I didn't admit that I quaked. I was still trying to straighten out my collar, but my fingers felt as thick and clumsy as corncobs.

The Shank stared on. He prided himself in knowing the name of every kid in the school, though it sometimes took him a while to get there. Not with me, though.

"Middleton," he said. "I want an explanation for this, and I want it now."

I cleared my throat.

"OK. Look, I admit I was in the toilets. Chilli last night – you know how it is. So, I heard someone come in. Whoever it was dumped these little guys on the floor. I was just checking them out when Tweedledumb and Tweedledumber came in. That's all there is to it."

Funt tensed next to me. I guessed I was going to pay

later for that crack. I considered it money well spent.

"And why should I believe this … *fairy tale* of yours?"

"It's no fairy tale."

"Are you familiar with Occam's Razor?" said the Shank in a different tone. It was almost friendly.

"Is that the barber's shop on the High Street?"

The Shank's mouth twitched. He managed to squeeze a lot of meaning into that twitch. The twitch said, *You are an idiot*, but then it corrected itself, and added, *Well, maybe not an idiot; maybe a smart alec. Either way,* the twitch said, *I don't like you. Don't like you at all.*

"Occam's Razor is the philosophical principle which dictates that where there are two competing explanations for a state of affairs, we should always choose the simpler."

"Clever guy, Occam," I replied. "But sometimes the simplest explanation is wrong. You know, some people think that this school is a dump simply because it's run by incompetents and crooks. But, personally, I think it's *way* more complicated than that."

I sensed a conflict raging within the Shank. He wanted to inflict some hurt. He wanted to inflict it *personally*. But that wasn't the deal.

"Bosola, Funt!"

"Sir?"

"I do believe our friend Middleton here is a little unwell. Take him along to the sick bay. Get him to lie down for a short while. We'll see if that improves his ... attitude."

Right, so now things really had taken a bad turn. The sick bay used to be just that: the place where you went to lie down after you'd puked. At one time there'd been a school nurse who'd take your temperature and paint your gums purple with iodine. Back when I first started to get ... *ill*, I'd hang out there sometimes, and the nurse would talk to me. She had tired eyes and sometimes you'd see her sitting alone in a cafe, smoking. But she was nice. And long gone. Now all that was left in the sick bay was a bucket of sand, and the sad remains of an old dummy used to initiate kids in the arcane rituals of artificial respiration.

But the sick bay had changed in one other, important way. It was now lined with padded material. In theory it was meant to protect kids who had fits in there, but its true function was, I knew, to make the room more or less soundproof. That meant no one could hear your screams, or the thuds as your head bounced off the walls.

* * *

So, I was to get a beating for my trouble. You could hear the smile spreading across Funt's face like a crack in a glacier.

The next thing I knew the big guy bent my arm behind my back and began marching me out of the Shank's office. He didn't get far. There was a brief knock, the door opened, and right there before us stood Mr Vole, headmaster of our school.

CHAPTER FOUR
ON THE CASE

VOLE had been reading a document as he walked in. Now he looked up. He was tall, but stooped, thereby nicely displaying the shiny top of his bald head. His pate was dimpled like a baby's bum, and was fringed by a circle of fine, white hair – hair that gave an impression of such infinitely soft downiness that it was impossible not to want to reach out and stroke it.

"Ah, er, yes, sorry, sorry, my apologies. I didn't realize that, so to speak, you were, I mean, er, busy. With these, ah, children, I mean pupils, which is to say, young people."

That's the way Vole spoke – he used up a lot of words to say not very much. He was also somewhat in awe of the Shank. No one was in awe of Vole. It would be like being in awe of a filing cabinet or an armchair.

"Not at all," said the Shank, grimly.

Then there was one of those silences for which the adjective *awkward* might have been invented. Vole looked from the Shank to Funt to Bosola and on to me, hoping that an explanation might emerge. His lips formed various words without committing any of them to the airwaves – I guessed that "er", "ah", "that is to say" and "in point of fact" were at least some of them.

Then Vole saw the brown twigs on the Shank's desk.

"Ah," he said, although this was a different sort of an "ah", one that had more poignancy and sadness in it. I'd guess, if pushed, you'd have to call it a sigh. He walked across the room and gazed at the tragic remains on the desk. His hands made a cupping motion, as if he were going to lift up the insects in a mute offering to the gods. But he didn't actually touch them.

He looked up. His eyes were moist.

"What … er, how did this … how did this *incident* … this *event* come to, ah, pass?"

"They were killed, sir," answered Bosola. "Murdered."

Vole looked uncomprehendingly at Bosola for a few moments. Then, as the truth sank in, he closed his eyes and brought his hands slowly together in front of his lips, as if in prayer.

"We try ... we try ... we try so hard. So very, very hard. We provide every and, ah, indeed any, opportunity to you young people, to the youth of ... ah, we give you every chance to flourish, to spread your legs, erm, which is to say, wings. And this is how you, ah, repay us. Truancy, theft, vandalism, destruction of school property ... animal cruelty. I wonder sometimes why we indeed, ah, bother." He opened his eyes again and looked at the Shank. "Why was I not informed of this?"

"I was just dealing with it," replied the Shank.

"But the death of ... the *demise* ... as you know, the school pet programme, well, it was *important* ... important to us all."

"Which is why I was giving it top priority."

"So who or what is, ah, responsible?"

The Shank raised his chin in my direction. "The finger points to this boy, Middleton. Two of my prefects caught him red-handed."

"It wasn't me," I blurted out. "I'm just the patsy, the fall guy. Wrong time, wrong place."

Vole's lips were wet. The rest of him was dry as a mummy's jock strap, but his lips were always moist, as if he'd been sucking the juice out of a watermelon. He licked them now.

"Mr Shankley seems to think that you were to blame. And these two boys appear to have witnessed, in the sense of, er, having seen the occurrence as it, ah, occurred."

"Sir, these two jokers didn't see a thing. They came in after the real killer had dumped the bodies. And," I added, letting a neat little pause hang in the air, "I think I know who it was."

"You're a liar, Middleton," said Bosola, menacingly. "You killed the bugs and you know it." He turned again to the Shank. "Just give us five minutes with him, sir. He'll confess, I guarantee you."

That threat turned out to be my lucky break. Vole wasn't much of a head teacher, but you couldn't call him brutal. He didn't turn a blind eye to all the violence in the place: he genuinely didn't see it. But even he couldn't miss Bosola's threat. Nor did he like the fact that a kid had just appealed over his head to someone who was supposed to be his deputy.

"I will not have that language in my, er, or anyone's office. In this, er, school, no man or woman, for that matter, let alone child, is guilty until it is proven that they are, which is to say that they are not, er, *innocent*. You, young man, Mandelson, was it…?"

"Middleton, sir."

"Right, Middlebum, you say you know who actually

committed this appalling act of, ah, *appallingness*."

"I think I do, sir."

"Kindly name the, ah, culprit."

I paused. The truth was that I had not the faintest idea who had killed the insects. I knew it wasn't me, but so far that was all the narrowing-down I'd done.

"I've no proof. I don't want to give you a name without hard evidence."

"The boy's bluffing. And wasting our time," snapped the Shank. "I suggest immediate suspension, followed, once we've established exactly what happened, by permanent exclusion."

"That seems to rather prejudge the, ah, issue..."

The Shank gave an exasperated sigh. "I wonder if we could discuss this for a moment in your office?"

"Well, naturally, you mean in private, of course, yes, yes."

The two of them went out into the corridor. Funt, Bosola and yours truly were left to puff and blow and look at the ceiling. After a minute or so, Funt aimed a casual kick at me. I caught his foot and held it, with the big dumb bozo tottering and yet frozen, like a photo of a tower block just after the demolition charges have gone off.

The Shank came back in and I let go of Funt's foot. I was expecting Vole to follow him, but he never showed.

That was a bad sign.

"You're a lucky boy," said the Shank. His face and his voice were neutral, unreadable. "Mr Vole seems to think that we haven't got the evidence to suspend you for this. Plus there is the issue of your ongoing … *problems*, and the fact that you've only recently returned from your period of … *recuperation*."

It should have been good news. Somehow I knew it wasn't.

"And so we're giving you four days – until Friday – to come back to us with a name."

"And if I don't?"

"Then we cancel the school play. What one might term a collective punishment."

I tried to work out the angle. I failed. "That's a shame, heck, it's a tragedy. But I don't act, can't sing, so why…?"

"And we let … *them* know that it's been cancelled because of you."

Them. That could only mean one thing.

The Queens.

Suddenly the room was very quiet. Quiet, that is, until Funt filled it with a bass guffaw, and Bosola with a falsetto giggle.

"You'll wish you'd been expelled," tittered Bosola.

That was the biggest case of stating the obvious

since the lookout on the Titanic yelled to mind the iceburg.

"We're done here, Middleton," said the Shank, and waved us to the door, his eyes already on the papers on his desk.

I was still too stunned to have a snappy answer ready, and I was halfway out the door before I remembered that there was something I would need if I were to stand a chance of pulling my ass out of the fire.

"I'll need a Warrant."

The Warrant was the official piece of paper issued to prefects and other kids on special duties. It gave you permission to go anywhere in the school any time you wanted.

"Don't push your luck, sonny," the Shank growled back. He used "sonny" in the same way as the Greek god Cronus used it, and he ate his kids alive.

"If you want the truth, then I need the paper."

The Shank thought for a moment, then opened a drawer and took out a neat stack of pre-printed A5 pages. He signed one with a fancy fountain pen and handed it to me.

"Don't make me regret this," he said, icily.

I was out of there just in time to hear the buzzer go for the end of the morning. Yeah, I'd been bluffing when I told Vole that I knew who'd done the deed on the sticks, but I meant to convert that bluff into a straight flush. And I knew exactly where to start looking.

CHAPTER FIVE
God Save The Queens

THE walk back to the toilets gave me the chance to think about the Shank's threat. It was bad. It was really bad. I was like a cow with a cut leg in the Amazon river, just waiting for the first piranha to get a sniff of the blood.

The Queens, or rather the Drama Queens, to give them their proper title, were the most powerful gang in the school. Their reach was longer, their grip tighter even than the prefects'. Their origins lay in the drama club that put on the twice-yearly school plays, but they'd grown beyond that. Way beyond.

To begin with, the Drama Queens had been a force for good. A refuge for all those out of step with the brutalities of everyday life in our school. For every star milking the lights out in front of the audience, there were twenty back-stage toilers: mousey, timid, but proud to play their part, however small, in the creation of something beautiful.

But then the drama club had been allocated a budget, and where there is money, corruption will grow, like mushrooms on a dung heap. Yeah, the Queens got greedy. Greedy first for the sake of their art and the prestige it brought them. But then just plain greedy.

The productions became more and more lavish. Stage sets began to grow, aping New York skylines or Indian jungles or Parisian ghettos as the show demanded. The orchestra swelled – we're not talking about three kazoos and a triangle here, but something big enough to put on Wagner's *Ring Cycle* with a side order of Bizet's *Carmen*. The costumes bloomed in gaudy extravagance. The stage was filled with light and glitter.

All very pretty, but it was never a good idea to get on the wrong side of the Queens. They looked after their own. If you messed with one Queen, you messed with them all. And if you got in the way of the juggernaut, then you were going to get crushed.

The Queens had fought a long turf war with the other main gang in the school, the Lardies. The Lardies were a sort of overweight mafia, and they controlled the supply of junk food to the kids who couldn't swallow the "healthy option" menu that the New Regime slopped onto their plates. The war between the Queens and the Lardies ended in a sort of compromise, with each gang finding a niche. But nobody doubted that the Queens had inflicted the deepest wounds. For now Hercule Paine, the leader of the Lardies, was content to lick those wounds. But revenge, as they say, is a dish best served cold, and then rammed down your enemy's throat so it chokes them to death.

Even though the Queens were now about much more than drama, drama was still at the centre of their world. Except that something rather strange had happened. Back in their glory days, the Drama Queens had put on two fresh shows every year. But now it was always the same two. The Christmas panto was *Cinderella*, and the summer show was *The Wizard of Oz*.

Oz, in particular, had become a kind of totem, a symbol. More than that, it was like those blood sacrifices performed by the Aztecs and other Mesoamericans. Without the offerings of hearts, the sun would not rise, the rains would not come, and the world would be lost to chaos and darkness. And without *Oz*, said the irrational beast that ravened in the school's subconscious, there would be equally terrible consequences. There would be a Ragnarok, the war at the end of time, and all kinds of bad shit would go down. That kind of thing.

Everyone knew that Shankley wanted the Drama Queens gone. The money and the power had put them out of his control. They needed to be destroyed. So far he hadn't had a good enough reason to close them down, but the death of the stick insects was just the pretext he needed.

And now I realized I was stuck in a web that a black widow would have been proud of. Funt and Bosola were sure to put the word around that I was the main suspect for the killing. The Shank had set this all up so that he couldn't lose. Either I found the perp, and he'd get the credit for solving the crime, or I failed, which would give him the excuse he wanted to fatally weaken the Queens by nixing the play. And nobody would blame him for zapping *The Oz*; it'd be me the Queens tied upside-down on the school gates, wearing nothing but a tutu and a feather boa, with a big "Q" drawn on my chest in pink lipstick.

Well, so far, the Queens and I hadn't had much to do with each other, but that was going to change.

First, though, I needed something to go on. A clue. And that meant returning to the crime scene.

CHAPTER SIX
CSI

THE toilets at lunchtime weren't quite as civilized as they were during lessons. The cubicles were all occupied. Some held Year Seven midgets, sobbing for their mothers. In some, grim rites were being performed: the ancient tortures of dunking and flushing. Others contained clandestine scoffers of the forbidden digestive biscuit or Mars bar. One cubicle had smoke pluming over it, although whether it was a furtive fag, or some kid setting himself on fire rather than face the school lunch, I couldn't say. Perhaps some of the cubicles were even being used for the purposes for which they were designed.

But my business wasn't with the cubicles, or the sad wretches they contained. Nor was it with the urinals – although I did briefly want to push a kid's face into the stinking bowl when I saw him spit his gum in there.

No, this wasn't the time for random acts of vigilantism. I was here because I remembered that metallic rattle, which meant that something had been dumped in the bin at the end of the row of sinks. I went straight to it and picked through the paper towels newly deposited there.

"Hey, psycho-boy, lost your pills?"

I looked up, but still fished around with my left hand. A couple of kids from my year loomed over me. Steve Wilson was one of the cool kids, if by cool you meant vain, shallow and asinine. His hair was greased into a quiff, and his tie-knot was the size of a baby's head. His friend was called Gamble or Grimble or some such, and he looked the same, with the minor handicap of a spray of acne like a meteor shower across his cheeks.

"I'm looking for your soul. I heard I could find it in the trash."

Wilson stared at me with a perplexed expression on his handsome, dumb face. "What the hell does that mean? If it's supposed to be funny, then it's not, and if it's supposed to be clever, then it's not. But if supposed to be lame, then you hit the jackpot."

Grimble or Gamble or whatever laughed through his nose, squirting a little snot.

On consideration, I thought Wilson was probably right. But I didn't care, because my fingers touched something hard and thin and long at the bottom of the bin. I reached round, found another and pulled them both out.

"What you got there, weirdo?" said Wilson, though this time there was genuine interest in his voice.

"Text me and I'll let you know," I replied as I walked out, hiding what I'd found under my blazer.

"You haven't even got a phone, nut-job," Wilson called after me as I swung the door shut in his face.

I went straight out into the Upper School playground. This was the set-up: the front of the school was for years seven–nine, the back of the school was for years ten and eleven. The Sixth Formers could go wherever they wanted, but usually just hung out in their common room. Any Lower School kid who strayed into the Upper School playground would be lucky to escape with nothing worse than a debagging, and any older kid who ventured into the realm of the Lower School would be mobbed and pelted and harried until he got the hell out.

But the side of the school was different. It was called the Interzone. It was a no man's land, where, in theory, anyone could go. It was also a dark and dangerous place. There were long fissures in between different school buildings where the sun never shone, folds and wrinkles in the school's skin, where lurkers lurked and shirkers shirked. This was where you'd find the goths and the emos, the psycho kids and the skins, the demented and the tormented. There was the corner where the Lardies ate their pies and currant buns. White-faced kids would gather round a Ouija board, or consult with some fake witch about love charms or wart cures. And deep in the dark heart of the Interzone was the foul and sordid alley where the Bacon-heads sought oblivion in their highly-processed, pig-flavoured drug of choice.

It hadn't always been like this. Before the New Regime, the Interzone was nothing more and nothing less than the side of the school. But Shankley's crackdown had forced all the seediest elements – as well as the innocent outsiders, anyone odd or freaky or just plain different – into that murky world. There they were left, boiled and sweated down to a toxic concentration, like tree-frog poison.

I began to walk towards the Interzone, but the Interzone wasn't my destination.

I had a pair of chopsticks in my hand with the initials L. M. on them, and I was headed for Chinatown.

CHAPTER SEVEN
CHINATOWN

CHINATOWN wasn't part of the Interzone, but it was as close as the "real" world came to that place of dreams and nightmares. Chinatown was the corner of the schoolyard bordering the Interzone. It wasn't like they had an ornamental arch there or dancing dragons. In fact, it was no more than four concrete benches, but it was where the Chinese kids hung out, and someone had given it the name and the name had stuck.

This wasn't my first visit to Chinatown. And it wasn't the first time I'd seen these chopsticks.

I'd noticed Ling Mei on my very first day at the school. I'd moved from out of town, and I hadn't met anyone Chinese before. She sat two rows in front of me, and even from behind I could tell she had something. Then she dropped her pencil, and somehow it rolled back to me, even though it should, by all the laws of physics, have rolled forwards. I bent and picked it up, and she reached back and smiled with her lips together, then looked down and then up again, still smiling. She was simultaneously demure and innocent, and hopelessly exotic. Her hair, so densely black you'd think it came from the heart of a dead star, was yet light enough to move in a breeze you could barely feel. The soft caramel of her skin was utterly flawless, so perfect, in fact, that you craved something – a mole or a freckle – to stop the heat of its perfection from burning your eyes out.

But I was twelve, and I could no more sweet-talk a girl than I could milk a yak. So it was two years before I finally asked her out for a coffee, and that was only because of the onions. We were working at the same bench in the domestic science class. We were making a Spanish omelette, and had to chop onions. Even then I hadn't said much, though my chest was beating as if some kind of big bird was in there, trying to flap its way out.

Then the onions got to work on our eyes. Soon there were tears streaming down our cheeks, and that seemed to release a heck of a lot of emotion, as if the causal chain between feeling and physical effect had been reversed. We were laughing – laughing *at* each other, laughing *for* each other – with the tears falling off our faces and splashing onto the work surface. And I saw something that gave me hope, and with hope, courage. I saw her teeth. Before that day I'd only ever seen that closed-mouth smile of hers, the one she'd blown my way on the first day of school. But now the lips opened, and there they were. White, of course. White and small and lovely. But one tooth – at the front on the left, in between the incisor and the canine – crossed over another. Crossed over it by the merest millimetre, but crossed just the same. She was *not* perfect. She was something beyond perfect, because utter perfection engenders within itself the flaw of unattainability.

"You drink coffee?" I asked, wiping the wet off my cheek.

She gave the tiniest little shake of her head, and suddenly her face was serious. There was a pause of maybe a second into which you could have fitted a couple of full-length operas, right down to the fat lady singing. Then the smile again – the one without the teeth.

"Tea."

I saw Ling Mei now, sitting with the other kids in Chinatown. They were eating noodles with chopsticks out of cardboard cartons, except for Ling Mei, who was using a plastic canteen fork. The moment I saw her, that bird came back to life in my chest, as I knew it would, flapping and squawking, like there was a fox in there chasing it. But today I wasn't here to moon around, yearning and dreaming. This wasn't one of the rainy nights I spent leaning against the lamppost outside her house, with my collar up and my hat brim down, hoping to prove my worth by sheer bloody perseverance, until her dad would come out with their Jack Russell terrier snarling at the end of its rope, and tell me to clear off before he called the police.

No, today I was here to find out why Ling Mei's chopsticks had hit the bin just after the stick insects had fallen like dry hail on the tiles of the toilet floor.

She turned just before I reached her. The smile flickered, then died, and she bent back to her noodles.

"Hey, Ling Mei."

I was too close to ignore.

"Hi," she said, as if I were a complete stranger.

I sensed the collective hostility of the group. Four guys and two other girls. I knew a couple of them by name. One I knew *too* well. Jimmy Tan had gone out with Ling Mei after me. He hated my guts. His guts I could take or leave.

"Not seen you use a fork before," I said.

"You think I don't know how?"

"I think you can do anything you set your mind to."

"So why do you care how I eat?"

Ling Mei sounded bitter. She sounded hurt. And I couldn't blame her, not after what I'd done. I put my hand on her shoulder.

"Look, Ling, I'm sorry—"

"This mental case bothering you, Ling Mei?"

That was Jimmy Tan.

"Butt out, Bruce," I said, without looking at him.

"It's OK, Jimmy," said Ling Mei. "I can handle this." Then she looked at me again, her face like an angel with bad news. "Just tell me what you want, John. Then go, please. Just go."

I took the chopsticks out of my pocket.

"I found these."

Her eyes opened wide, but she didn't say anything.

"You hear about the stick insects?"

I guessed that word had gotten round. It's what word did, at our school.

She nodded, and a tiny cloud passed over her face.

"I was there when it happened. In one of the cubicles." Suddenly I wasn't happy with the picture that might have formed in her beautiful head. "I mean just sitting out maths, like you do."

"I don't," she said.

"Yeah, well, we can't all be geniuses. Anyway, I heard someone dump the bodies. Then whoever did it threw these in the bin. That's where I found them."

I handed the chopsticks to her.

She looked at them for a moment, then up at me, as what I was saying sank in. Her face found an expression I'd never seen there before. It was one part outrage, one part anger, one part huge sadness.

"What are you saying? That I did this? You're saying I killed those poor creatures? With my chopsticks? You're a—" And then she said some bad words; first some bad English words, and then, when she'd used them up, some bad Chinese words.

Before I had the chance to say anything back, I sensed a movement off to the side. It was Jimmy. He was reaching behind his back. I knew what was coming next: I was going to be staring at two pieces of heavy wood, joined by a short length of chain – a nunchaku, called the numchuck by idiots. In either case, a serious piece of hardware. I was guessing that Jimmy's nunchaku would be Okinawa style: instead of being rounded like a broom handle, the wood was octagonal, the sharp edges designed to inflict maximum damage.

I took a step back and got into my fighting stance. Then I saw something glinting in the fingers of another of the Chinese kids. Tony Yu. We had a couple of classes together. He was OK. OK, that is, when he wasn't holding a hira-shuriken, better known as a Ninja death star.

This wasn't looking good.

"I'm not here to fight you, Jimmy," I said. "But I will, if I must."

And then I noticed that the expressions on their faces changed.

"He thinks he's Jackie Chan," said someone.

Another kid sliced the air with a couple of comedy karate chops.

Laughter. Hard, mocking laughter. Maybe they were hiding their fear. Maybe they were just laughing.

Then from his backpack Jimmy pulled out, not a nunchaku, but a banana. The hira-shuriken in Tony Yu's hand turned into a coin that he tossed in the air, caught and tossed again.

Suddenly my head hurt, and I had that feeling you get sometimes, you know, like when you put a T-shirt on back to front, and realize that something's wrong, but you can't put your finger on it.

"OK, get lost, you're putting me off my dessert," said Jimmy. And then he threw the banana peel in my face.

That was enough. I'd taken a lot of crap today. It was time to hand some out.

"STOP!"

It was Ling Mei.

She was talking to the Chinese kids. "He can't help it. He's been … he's not…"

Then she swivelled and she was suddenly right in my face.

"My chopsticks were stolen from my bag this morning. You get that? Stolen! I had nothing to do with the death of those things, nothing. If you ever thought I did, ever thought I could, then it means you never knew me, never cared for me, never – never…" And then she trailed off, because she knew that if she carried on, then she would lose control completely, and the world would see her weep.

I thought about taking Ling Mei's hand, but something told me the time for holding hands was gone.

"Look," I said, fighting to keep my voice steady, "if I don't find out who did this, the Shank is going to cancel the *Wiz*, and tell the Queens it was down to me."

Jimmy laughed and drew his hand across his throat.

"You want white or red roses on your grave?" said Tony.

I ignored them. "I never thought you had anything

to do with it, Ling Mei. I just wanted to know who could have taken the chopsticks. It's the only clue I've got."

She looked at me, her beautiful face red and puffy from the suppressed tears. The fire of hatred had burned out, as hatred that comes from lost love always will.

"Anyone in my registration class could have taken them. Or anyone who bumped into me in the corridor afterwards."

Great. That narrowed it down to pretty well the entire population of the school.

"You should go now," she added.

I looked at Tony Yu and Jimmy Tan and the other Chinese kids, their faces either blank or hostile or scornful.

She was right.

I went.

CHAPTER EIGHT
A Dangerous Lady

SO, I'd gained a faceful of banana skin and lost my dignity. But that's the truth of Chinatown: you take something away, you leave something behind. And you never know who's going to get the best of the bargain.

I sat on a bench and put my collar up against the cold wind. Then I fished around inside my brain, hoping to pull out a good one. My only lead had been the chopsticks, but it had melted like a prawn cracker on my tongue. Ling Mei had nothing to do with this, and she couldn't help me train a spotlight on the perp.

What did that leave?

A football rolled towards the bench. I punted it back to the players, without getting up.

Nothing.

No, not nothing. I still had a pocket full of stick insects, and I knew where they had come from. I got up and walked back to the main school building.

"Where you going?"

A hand was on my chest, pushing me back.

"I'm doing a job for the Shank."

"If you mean 'Mr Shankley', say Mr Shankley."

There were two prefects on duty at all the doors. These two punks were just going through the motions. One had fat lips and goofy teeth and looked like he was auditioning for the role of Village Idiot. The other, the talker, stank of cheap cigarettes and urine. *Cheap urine.* He'd obviously just dipped into the Interzone for a smoke, and maybe sat in a puddle of something unpleasant. Maybe he'd brought his own puddle with him.

I pulled the Warrant out of my pocket and shoved it in the prefect's face.

"Tell it to the Chief," I said, and walked through them like they weren't there.

I trudged up the stairs and along corridors ripe with the tang of unwashed kids, until I reached the science department.

I looked through the toughened glass window of

the biology lab. Mrs Maurice was right there at her desk. She looked like she was marking papers. Her hair was up and she had on her reading glasses. There was a cardigan draped over her shoulders and a pencil in her mouth. Only the shiny apple was missing to complete the picture of the perfect schoolmistress.

But the image was as misleading as a party hat on a panther. Mrs Maurice was deadly, and I gulped twice before I knocked on that door.

"Come," she said, without looking up. I knew why she did that, and it had nothing to do with her being engrossed in the biology paper she was marking. You see, Mrs Maurice looking up was a thing to behold, a thing of rehearsed, theatrical accomplishment that could be almost operatic in its impact. And she wasn't going to waste it until her audience had settled.

So, it wasn't until I was in the room that she put down her pencil and slowly unfurled herself. In one sinuous, silky movement, she slid off her glasses and shook out her lustrous hair. As her face rose, she slowly opened those huge, dark eyes. So slowly, in fact, you'd think they'd never get there. And in a way you'd be right, because her eyes always did look as if they were in the act of closing again, as if she was in the first dreamy stages of a kiss.

And if you think that all makes Mrs Maurice sound

like a honey, you'd be right. And dead *wrong*.

Despite the fact that she had the power to make the world see her in soft focus, there were moments when you got a glimpse of reality. If she waited a little too long in between Botox injections, the lines around her mouth and eyes would reappear. At the end of a long day, her skin would lose its lustre and her eyes their depth. And one girl swore blind that she'd once seen a millimetre of a grey hair that was almost white at the roots.

That girl might have been lying, but even if it were true, Mrs Maurice was still an awful lot of woman for one kid to handle.

"Hello, *Johnny*," she said, making my name sound slightly obscene, the way she always did. I'd been in her class a couple of years before and she knew me pretty well. "It's been such an awfully long time since I had you up in my lab."

I coughed. I blushed. I coughed and blushed some more.

"I'm here on business," I said. Actually, what I said was "I'm here on b–b–business."

"Business?" Mrs Maurice smiled the word rather than said it. "What sort of business?"

I walked the rest of the way to her desk.

"This sort of business."

I emptied Funt's hanky full of dead stick insects over the exam paper she was marking.

She was not an easy lady to shock.

"Oh, I was wondering when they would turn up again."

"You knew they were missing?"

She turned her pout up to eleven, and said in a little-girl-playing-with-dolls voice: "Of course I knew they were missing. They were my babies."

It was creepy and cute in about equal measure.

"When did they go walkabout?"

"I really couldn't say for sure. I didn't get in until late today. By the time I came up from the staffroom it was, let me see" – she sucked thoughtfully on her pencil, and I fought to stop my eyes from going crossed – "half past eleven—"

"And they were gone?"

"And they were gone."

"Was the door to the lab locked?"

Mrs Maurice gave me a long look, one that I'd have had to be about a thousand years older to fully understand, and said, "Oh, Johnny, you know very well that I have an open-door policy."

Focus. I had to keep focused.

"And you've no idea who might have, er, murdered the insects?"

"You mean did anyone have a grudge against them?" She stretched her sleepy eyes wide, mimicking fright.

I was getting nowhere. Time to try absolute honesty and seriousness.

"Look, Mrs Maurice, I'll level with you. I'm here because the Shank…"

She raised an eyebrow. It was a neat trick. Not her only one.

"I mean Mr Shankley. He thinks I've got something to do with all this. I was in the toilets when the sticks got dumped. He wants my head on a spike. And it's not just me. The Shank wants the whole school to suffer for this – he's gonna cancel the school play unless we get it sorted out. So, if you've any ideas…"

That eyebrow headed north again. I don't think she could stop it if she tried.

"About these guys, I mean…" I pointed down at the dry, brown bodies.

"Why don't we ask one?" said Mrs Maurice. She picked one of the insects up and whispered to it. Then she held it up to her ear, and nodded and gasped a little.

"What does he say," I asked, resigned.

"She."

"What?"

"It's a she. They're all ladies. She says—" And then, all of a sudden, she stopped the play-acting. Maybe she took pity on me. Maybe she got bored. Or maybe I was suddenly seeing the world straight. Anyway, for a second she looked ten years older. "Look, John," she said, sounding like any other teacher, "I haven't a clue what happened. You're a good kid and I'd like to help you, but I don't see how I can. The stick insects were here, then they weren't. Now they're back again and dead. That's all I know."

"Can you at least tell me how they died? I mean they don't seem to have been squished or anything."

"What, you want me to do an *autopsy*?"

I shrugged. She sighed.

"Leave them with me," she said.

"Thanks," I said, and left.

CHAPTER NINE
A History Lesson

I had to hurry to make it to my afternoon class. It was history, taught by Mr Hemp. Hemp was the right man for the job – he was a thousand years old and as arid as the Gobi Desert. There was no period in history that he couldn't suck the life out of.

The class was still getting settled, but Hemp was already speaking. It sounded like he'd been gargling chalk again. He pronounced every word quite separately, as if it were utterly alone and unconnected with any other. The effect of this was that, although the meaning of each word might be clear, it was impossible to keep a track of the general gist:

"And. The. Athenians. Overreached. Themselves. When. In. The. Midst. Of. Their. War. With. The. Spartans.

And. Goaded. Into. Action. By. Alcibiades. Whose. Desecration. Of. The. Sacred. Herms. Prevented. His. Own. Participation. They. Launched. An. Invasion. Of. Sicily …"

As I sat down, I realized that the class was silent and staring.

I felt a jab in my back. I resisted the urge to turn round.

"Why did you do it, Middleton?"

I recognized the voice of pretty-boy Steve Wilson.

"What did you kill them for? You do it for fun? Cos you're sick? Cos you're a wacko? You shouldn't be in a normal school. You should be with the other mental kids in the nut house."

I heard the scrape of a chair. I could see what was coming. Wilson was leaning forward to slap the back of my head. He was that kind of kid. Well, this time he'd chosen the wrong head to slap. I ducked, and felt the swish of a hand passing through my hair. And now that he was off balance, it was easy work to catch his wrist, pull him forwards over his desk and roll him onto the floor. Easy work, but slickly done, even if I say so myself.

There was a guffaw from the class – the fickleness of the mob is the one thing you can always rely on – and Hemp looked round from the board, where he'd been writing down ten key facts about his friends, the Athenians.

"What is the meaning of this?"

"Wilson just overreached himself, sir," I replied.

Hemp blinked at me. I guessed that his mind was away on some remembered or imagined archaeological dig, back when he was young and still full of the excitement of discovery. There he was, trowel in hand, scraping away the soil from a bone or a pottery shard, and suddenly I'd dragged him back to this classroom full of kids who didn't want to learn. And it turned out that his lonely life had slipped by, and now he was old and half dead with nothing achieved.

"I–I..." said Hemp, his voice like the rustle of dry leaves in a hot breeze. And then he lost his way, and nothing followed.

I suddenly felt sorry for the old fossil and wished I'd found a better way of humiliating that jerk Wilson than disrupting the class.

But before Mr Hemp had the time to find the right word to come after "I", the door opened. Only after he'd opened it did the kid bother to knock, and the knock was a kind of satire, a reminder of its own impertinent absence, like a pretty girl blowing you a kiss after she'd just told you to get lost.

The class turned to the newcomer, like Wimbledon spectators following the ball.

He was tall and willowy and wore his hair long.

His face was as perfect and as blank as a Byzantine Madonna. His name was Hart, and he was a Drama Queen.

The kid called Hart spoke to Hemp. Spoke to Hemp, but looked at me.

"I've come for Middleton," he said, sounding bored. "Drama business." Hart wore a black feather boa threaded through the belt loops of his trousers.

It was accepted throughout the school that in the couple of weeks leading up to a big production, "drama business" came first, and kids could get called out of lessons at any time.

"Take him," said Hemp, glad, I think, to be relieved of one more burden.

"What's this all about?" I asked Hart, although I had a pretty good idea.

We were heading towards the drama studio. The shows took place in the main hall, but the studio was the Drama Queens' Kremlin.

"She'll tell you when we get there."

No need to tell me who "she" was.

"Because, you know, if it's a Dorothy you want, I'd have learned the lines," I said.

Suddenly that perfect, expressionless face was contorted with something like rage.

"There's only one Dorothy in this school," hissed Hart, "and it's not you."

Again, there was no need to ask who the one, true Dorothy was.

"OK, don't get your boa in a twist. I was just making conversation."

"Sure," said Hart, and once again his words sounded like they could hardly be bothered to crawl out of his lips. "Me too."

The drama studio was on the top floor. I was breathing heavily by the time we got there, but Hart looked like he'd done nothing more taxing than caressing his hair out of his face. Turns out that the combo of modern dance and high drama can keep you pretty fit.

Hart pushed open the door and stood back as I entered.

The studio was well sound-proofed, so the noise and bustle hit me with the surprise of a wet fish in the face. There were, maybe, twenty jabbering Year Seven kids in a straggling line. Year Sevens always look like they could ride to school on cats, but these were the smallest of the small. I suppose it's because they were—

"MUNCHKINS!"

The scream came from a commanding figure,

entering from stage left. "Scream" gets it wrong. Right for volume, wrong for tone. Scream is what you do when you lose control because of fear or fury. But this was controlled, directed and lethal. It came from a Dorothy, but a Dorothy unlike any you've ever seen.

"MUNCHKINS!"

Things had mellowed down from fog-horn level to mere holler.

The milling Munchkins fell into a terrified silence.

"You see I *thought* we were doing *The Wizard of Oz*. This is *supposed* to be the yellow brick road and you are meant to be Munchkins. But it looks to me as though you've decided that you don't like *The Wizard of Oz*. It looks to me like you've decided on something different. It looks to me as if we're doing *The Pied Piper of Hamelin* and you lot are nothing but a bunch of filthy, stinking, plague-ridden

RATS!"

The last word had the sudden shocking impact of a German 88 mm anti-tank round, and a couple of the Munchkins actually fell over.

I couldn't decide if the whole thing were grotesquely comic, or just plain grotesque. Either way, a grin licked at the corners of my mouth.

And then things took a more sinister turn. Dorothy grabbed one of the Munchkins by the ear.

"I don't think you're listening to me, are you?"

The Munchkin writhed and emitted a pitiful keening noise, like some small rodent in the jaws of a weasel.

"You know what happens to Munchkins who don't listen?"

The Munchkin squealed again, as Dorothy applied an extra twist.

"No? Then I'll tell you."

Then Dorothy whispered in the Munchkin's ear, the one she was still twisting. The child's legs buckled, and it was only that relentless ear-grip that kept him off the floor. The kid begged Dorothy for mercy, using inchoate sounds rather than actual words. She let go and he fell to his knees.

It was sick and I wanted it to stop. But it was Hart who acted. He went over and spoke to Dorothy. Dorothy spun towards him, her eyes blazing fire. I thought she was going to strike or scratch, but then she controlled herself, glanced over towards me, and smiled a smile that could have blasted King Kong off the top of the Empire State Building.

"Well," she said in a voice like honey drizzled over rotting plums, "aren't you a nice-looking boy, for a killer."

I smiled and acknowledged the compliment with a brief blush.

"Let's go and talk in my dressing room."

This wasn't the first time I'd seen Emma West, better known as Dorothy, but it was the first time she'd spoken to me. She was at the top of the pile in our school, and she'd earned it the hard way. The Queens were what they were today because of her. She'd found them in complete disarray and forged them into the disciplined fightin'-and-dancin' machine they had become.

There was a disconcerting ambiguity to Emma West, almost as if she were a boy who looked like a girl playing at being a boy impersonating a girl. You wouldn't call her beautiful, or even pretty – her features were too heavy for that – but she pulled at your eyes like a peacock, and she could sashay for England.

The dressing room was through a door at the back of the studio. It was obviously designed to perform various technical functions, and it was still lined with assorted pieces of audio-visual equipment – the light-controller, a sound mixer, and other stuff I didn't understand. However, the whole place had been transformed with cushions and drapes and random pieces of fabric, and the air was heavy with perfume and powder.

It was also full of Drama Queens. Some were in costume – there a couple of witches, one wicked, the other very wicked. There was a Tin Man and a Scarecrow. Other Queens were in their school uniforms. And they were staring at me with exactly the mixture of suspicion and hunger that the lions in the zoo reserved for the hunk of meat just tossed over the fence.

The Queen Mother threw herself down on a long, backless couch, raised at one end. What was it – a *chaise longue*? An ottoman? I couldn't remember, but it was a decadent thing to have in a school like ours. Anyway, she lay across the ottoman – we'll settle on ottoman – like a python, a python with curves instead of coils, and I stood in front of her like Mowgli before Kaa.

She stretched out a hand and a tall, thin glass appeared in it. It was full of bubbles.

She looked at me again, and I couldn't hold her gaze. Those eyes had seen too much.

"You know why you're here," she said at last.

Question or statement? I wasn't sure.

"I guess you've heard about the stick insects," I ventured.

"You guess right."

"And that I was mixed up in it."

"Go on."

"And that unless I find out who did the deed, the play – *your* play – gets cancelled."

I felt the room's hostility level rise like the water when a fat man gets into the bath.

"Get one thing straight, pretty boy," said Emma. "*Nothing's* going to stop this show."

"Then maybe you should help me find out what's really going on here."

"And how do you propose I do that?"

"I'm just a guy on his own. You've got the resources; you've got the reach. There's not much that goes on in this school that the Queens don't know or couldn't find out about. If we work together, we can crack this."

"But the entire world seems to think that you're the one behind it. In fact, there is a very easy way to sort this out right now. You run along to Mr Shankley, and you tell him that you killed those itty-bitty bugs for whatever crazy motive you had. Then you take your punishment and the play goes on. Simple."

"Not so simple. I didn't do it."

Dorothy sighed. "I'm bored with this. I've got Munchkins to train. We tried playing nice, Middleton. We tried giving you a chance."

And suddenly I found, as she was speaking, that there were hands gripping me. No single hand was strong, but together they were overpowering. I was set down on the floor and held like a pirate about to have his leg sawn off.

"Sophie!"

I heard the door open and felt a heavy tread. Whatever it was that just came in was standing out of sight behind me. Suddenly I was freaked – and it takes quite a lot to freak me. Somehow I knew that behind me there lurked something truly terrible, something from the depths of the earth – or perhaps just from the darkest place of my subconscious.

"Yes, Dorothy?" The voice squeaked like Minnie Mouse, but this was one of those occasions when you know the voice doesn't go with the mouth.

"Playtime."

Giggles. Girlish giggles.

Sweat burst out on my forehead, and I strained to see whatever it was that moved behind me.

But I couldn't see. I would never see.

"Look," I said, panic giving my voice a metallic edge. "The Shank has given me four days. That's all I need. I'll find the real killer, and then everyone gets to go to the Emerald City."

"If I let Sophie loose on you, you'll say whatever I tell you to say, do whatever I tell you to do."

"Then that makes you worse than the Shank. Even he was prepared to give me some time to get to the bottom of this."

Dorothy came so close I thought she was going to

kiss me. But I saw something in her eyes. She was ruthless and she was powerful, but she wasn't the Shank.

"So, what if I trust you and you let me down, huh?"

"I won't let you down."

"That's what you boys always say."

"If I don't find the real killer in four days, then I'll take the fall. I'll be your patsy."

Again Emma West stared at me with those ageless, beautiful, fatal eyes. I could have been waiting for three seconds or three hours.

"OK, you've got your chance."

I heard a stunted wail of disappointment from behind, and heavy steps moved away. The hands holding me released their grip, and I picked myself up from the floor.

"I think Sophie liked you," said Emma, conjuring up the image of a whale liking krill. "And if you don't find out who did this, then I guarantee you'll be getting better acquainted."

I shrugged. "If I get out of this maybe you and I can give Sophie the opportunity to feel a little jealous."

Emma laughed. It was the first sound I'd heard coming out of her mouth that seemed spontaneous. Suddenly she looked like what she was: a drama-crazed schoolgirl who just wanted to put on a show.

"Maybe, kid, maybe," she said. She flickered close to me, like a flame, and kissed my cheek. "Don't make me sorry. You won't like it."

And then she spun away on her kitten heels, and I headed for the corridor.

On the way, I felt a hand on my sleeve. It was Hart.

"You want to know where to look?" he asked, in that careless way of his, as though nothing mattered.

I wasn't in the mood for him, or for cryptic questions.

"Get screwed, Hart," I said. "I don't care by who or what so long as I don't have to watch."

He sighed a little. "Some people you just can't help."

I wanted to inflict a little pain on Hart, but the truth was I had nothing. "Say what you've got to say."

"The Lardies."

Then he was gone. And so was I.

CHAPTER TEN
A Cat, a Dog, a Cold Welcome

THERE was only half an hour of the school day left, so I slipped through the gates and began walking home. It was a mile. A long mile. I'd been slapped, punched, kicked and coshed. I was sad and sore and confused.

And hungry: I'd had nothing to eat all day.

The streets around the school were pretty scuzzy. In places, low-rise concrete blocks had replaced the old redbrick houses, but they in turn were now being demolished, leaving scruffy open spaces where people had once lived out their lives. Nothing lived there now, unless you counted the odd hunched rat. In one of these dead zones a gang of skeletal children stood around a burning mattress. You could see the stains on the mattress, like archaeological layers: the incontinence of childhood; the marks of love or lust; the returning incontinence of dotage. And now the smoke and stench of the pyre.

One of the kids stooped to pick up a piece of broken brick. He hurled it at me, but it fell short, and he returned his gaze to the smoking mattress. I walked further, then turned back, but all I could see was the smoke and haze, and I wondered if I had imagined the skeletons and the brick.

A little further on I heard a racket. Furious barking, hissing, yowls. I looked around. The council had planted a few feeble saplings here and there to create the illusion that they cared about the environment. Most had been ripped up or kicked down or just plain poisoned by the rotten air. But a few remained. And now a skinny black cat was perched a couple of metres up one of them, and a dog was leaping at it, its jaws snapping just below the leafless branch.

The dog was some kind of cyborg killing-machine. Not pure pit bull, but pit bull mixed with the meanest genes from the meanest dogs. The cat was as high up as it could go in the flimsy tree and the dog was going insane. It frothed at the mouth and its eyes were filled with hate and death lust.

I thought about walking on. Did, in fact, for a couple of steps. But then I turned. The cat was going to be dog food, and I didn't want that on my conscience. The trouble was that I couldn't see how I could help without getting myself chewed up too.

I walked towards the dog. It was still in psycho mode and had started to bite its way through the slender trunk of the sapling. Either it had worked out that if it could chomp through the wood, it would get the cat, or it was just in the mood to bite anything that got in range.

"Easy, boy," I said, in a soothing voice.

The dog stopped chewing the tree, looked at me for a second, then got back to work. You could almost see the thought going through its head: *Cat first, then him.*

I walked closer. It really was a beast of a dog. There was definitely some Rottweiler in there. Japanese Tosza probably too. Heavy muscles rippled around its neck like waves in lava. Every nerve in my body was screaming at me to run. But sometimes you have to slap yourself in the face, grit your teeth and go on.

There was a splintered piece of wood on the floor. I picked it up and waved it in front of the dog. It stopped chewing the tree again; its black eyes followed the movement, back and forth, back and forth.

"OK, boy, fetch," I yelled, and gave the stick a mighty hurl. I couldn't believe my luck when the dog bounded after it. I quickly went up to the tree, expecting to have all kinds of trouble coaxing the cat down. But as soon as I put my hands up to it, the little creature leapt into my arms. It wormed its way into my jacket, and trembled, light as an autumn leaf. It was so insubstantial it hardly seemed to exist at all.

The dog was still busy killing the stick, but it wouldn't be long until he remembered that cat tastes better than wood, so I legged it in the opposite direction down the street, going at a lick to give Usain Bolt a scare. I imagined the beast tearing after me, jumping onto my back, its solid bulk forcing me down, the huge teeth sinking into the nape of my neck. But for a change, the worlds of imagination and reality stayed separate, and I reached my front door unsavaged.

I put the cat down on the doorstep. I thought it would slink away, but it coiled itself around my legs, purring like it was running off an electric motor.

"Sorry, Cat, you can't come in. My mum's allergic."

But the purr began to sound so much like "please" that I gave in.

"OK, I'll feed you, but then you're gone. There's probably some kid out there who's missing you already."

I opened the door on a house as empty as a skull. I'd forgotten that they'd all gone to the funeral. My eye went to the cork noticeboard:

Johnny, remember to take your medication.

That irritated me. Why couldn't they just trust me? I scrunched the note and slam-dunked it into the bin.

"OK, Cat," I said, "let's get you something to eat."

I found a can of sardines.

"Who the hell eats sardines?" I wondered aloud.

"Meeeeee," mewed the cat.

"Come on then; let's do this on the roof. You'll like it."

I had the attic room, which suited me fine. There was a dormer window sticking out from the slope of the roof. It wasn't a tough job to climb out and sit up there, on the flat of the dormer. I took the cat and the sardines out with me. She sniffed at the edge of the roof nervously, but then relaxed. I opened the can and before I put it down, she was greedily lapping at the oil.

"Hungry, eh?"

She was too busy eating to answer.

The roof was my favourite place to be in all the world. Nothing could reach me here. It was pure and free.

Except that thoughts of the day crept in, feeler-first, like cockroaches.

There was something I was missing. Something not quite right. Aside, I mean, from the massacre of the stick insects and the various beatings I'd taken.

I tried to get the universe to come into focus. But it was like when you stare at a light bulb and then look away, and the yellow image of the bulb is superimposed on whatever you're looking at. Except this was as though I'd been staring at a light bulb in the shape of the world, and the light-bulb world was now lying over the real world, but was shifted out of sync by a degree or two.

I got lost in that thought for a while, the thought of the different worlds, one made out of light and one made of earth, and then when that got me nowhere, I scrolled through the memory tapes a few more times, pausing at the key events.

Funt and Bosola.

The Shank.

Vole.

Chinatown.

Mrs Maurice.

The Queens.

I tried fitting them together this way and that, but all I got was the jabber of modern jazz played by a deaf Bulgarian.

Hungry. I'd forgotten that I was hungry. And I had to take my pills. The cat had licked the tin clean. I tried to pick her up to bring her back in, but she slid through my hands. Then she jumped down nimbly onto the balcony on the floor below, from there leapt to the garage roof, and then was lost in the twilight.

"Bye, then," I said, and heard an answering purr from the shadows down below.

In the kitchen I opened a tin of peaches. Some people thought it was weird that all I ever seemed to eat was tinned peaches. But I have a dark secret: I like tinned peaches.

I crashed down on the sofa and tried to shut out the events of the day. I tried to pretend that it was all make-believe, a fantasy. It worked, and I was half-asleep when the phone rang.

"Hi, Johnny."

I was still groggy. For a second I thought it might be Ling Mei. I saw her face, but then it dissolved into Emma West. But that wasn't right either. It was...

"Hello, Mrs Maurice."

"Hey, Johnny. I've been thinking about you. And your little friends."

"How did you get this number?"

"I'm your teacher, Johnny. There are all kinds of things I know about you."

I didn't want to get caught up in one of *those* conversations with Mrs Maurice, so I cut to the chase.

"Did you find out what happened to the sticks?"

There was a pause. I could hear her breathing into

the receiver. Then she answered, and her voice was cool and professional.

"I believe I did, yes. You see, there was something about this incident that puzzled me. The stick insects had been killed and then thrown onto the floor in the lavatory block. That all suggested some random act of violence. But I couldn't find a mark on the bodies. If this was some little brat's idea of a jape, some spur-of-the-moment thing, then you'd have expected him – or her – to squash the stick insects. But they'd been killed without violence."

"Killed by a pacifist. Nice irony."

"Quite. Though perhaps I should have said without *undue* violence. And that requires a certain amount of expertise. There are various ways of killing bugs without damaging them. You can suffocate them. You can freeze them. Or you can poison them."

"And how did these guys meet their end?"

"I've already told you, these weren't guys. You see the phasmids – that's the stick insects and their relations – usually reproduce by parthenogenesis. That is to say the females do not need to … *mate* in order to produce fertile eggs."

"*Jeez*, another reason not to be a stick insect."

You know how sometimes you can *hear* a smile? I heard one now.

"So," she continued, "we've finally found something we agree on."

There was a danger of veering off-piste. I took us back onto a blue run.

"Mrs Maurice, what killed the stick insects?"

"Ethyl acetate. Harmless to humans, but deadly to invertebrates."

I was impressed.

"How did you trace it?"

"Well, you can use a combination of a custom-designed ion mobility spectrometer with an ultra-violet ionization source and a high-speed capillary column. That will pick up a range of volatile organic compounds, including acetone and ethyl acetate. Or you can … sniff."

"What?"

"Do you remember the faint smell that the stick insects gave off?"

"Yeah, vaguely…"

"Recognize it?"

I shook my head, which is always a little futile when you're on the phone. Then I had a vision. My mother getting ready to go out. Sitting in front of her dressing table, draped in towels. Using little pads of cotton wool to clean the old nail varnish off, leaving a clean canvas for the shiny new coating of red.

"Nail polish remover," I said.

"Precisely. The active ingredient of which is—"

"Let me guess: ethyl acetate."

"Good boy."

"So," I said, thinking aloud, "we've got someone who, for whatever reason, didn't want to mash up the bugs, and who had access to some nail varnish remover—"

"Which means almost anyone."

"Yeah, OK. Anyone who paints their nails. But it's something to go on. I don't know how to thank you, Mrs Maurice."

"Oh," she said, innocently, "I'm sure if you tried really, *really* hard you could come up with something."

"I'll bring you an apple."

"It's a deal. Good night."

"Good night."

I flicked through the TV channels. Nothing but garbage, so I climbed back upstairs and out onto my roof.

The evening was clear, but the red hum of light from the city wiped out most of the stars. Just one big, bright planet glowed low down, to the south. Too big and yet too dull for flashy Venus. Jupiter, I guessed, screwing his way through the cosmos. And then I heard a mewling growl, and the cat was there.

"Hey, Cat," I said.

I was happy she'd come back. She stuck her claws into me with delicate spite as she climbed up onto my lap. She licked her paws and cleaned her face and then melted warmly into me. I felt along the wall behind me for the little box I kept my cigarettes in. I'd started coming up here because my parents would have gone ape if they'd caught the smell of smoke in my room. I lit the cigarette, lay back and blew smoke into the empty night, and thought about nothing, nothing at all.

That night I dreamed I was a defenceless stick insect. I was the last one. The others had all been crushed. And whatever had crushed them was after me. I was doped up on – what was it? – ethyl something. My stick legs moved so slowly. My stick body swayed and trembled with each laborious step. There was a shadow. I looked up. It was coming. It was huge. It was pink.

I woke up drenched in sweat, but then drifted off again, remembering too late about my meds.

DAY TWO
WEDNESDAY

CHAPTER ELEVEN
The Girl

FOR the first six minutes of school the next day everything was normal. I'd walked through the heavy drizzle, and made it through the gates and into the school building. I'd gone down two corridors, and hadn't yet been strangled, coshed or vamped. I was standing in front of my locker, ready to retrieve the PE kit I'd stuffed in there, still damp and grimy from the week before.

My locker was number 526. It was at the end of the row. The two lockers next to mine – 525, and the one next to that, 524 – had always been vacant. I guess it was a cordon sanitaire, a quarantine zone, to make sure nobody caught whatever it was I had.

Well, now someone was in the zone. Close enough to catch it…

I could tell, even from the side, that she was a stunner. Her features had a calm, almost grave perfection, brilliantly counterpointed by the fact that she was more pierced than Saint Sebastian. Ears, nose and eyebrow I could see: the rest was speculation, although I was prepared to put real money down on her tongue. She was tall in a way that hovered just on the right side of gangly. She had purple nails and purple lips and there was tragedy in her eyes, as if they'd seen bad things. Seen them, forgotten about them, then remembered them again.

I shovelled my crusty sports gear into my bag, hoping that the faint puff of malodorous gas didn't reach her in exchange for the delicate and decadent aroma of violets and smoke she was sending my way.

I'm a guy who prefers to work to a plan. I can improvise a melody, but I like the rhythm track laid down nice and solid. So I quickly formulated one. I'd glance over in her direction. Then, if she glanced back, I'd give her a smile. I went through a few of my smile options:

There was sardonic.

There was conspiratorial.

There was sexy.

There was the smile that said, *Hey, I'm deep, but I also have a good sense of humour.*

There was a smile that said, *Stick with me, babe, and I'll show you a heck of a good time.*

And then there was goofy.

My fear was that I'd go for sardonic or sexy and hit on goofball by mistake, like a prospector striking fool's gold. Anyway, if she answered my smile with a smile, then I'd ask her a question. And if she said yes, then we'd be married in a week and spend the rest of our lives together in a cottage in the woods.

But when I finally got around to glancing at her, she was too focused on getting her key into her locker to notice. It looked like there was something wrong with the key. Or maybe the lock. Finally she rammed the key home and twisted.

I guess what she saw when she opened the door was supposed to make her scream.

Most kids would have screamed.

Not this one. If I hadn't already been looking at her, then I probably wouldn't have realized that something was happening. But I was looking, and so I saw her flesh freeze, saw her body become utterly rigid, saw the fine bones in her face sharpen. She had the stillness you sometimes see in a spider, perched at the edge of its web, its long legs alive to the slightest movement of the threads. It was a stillness that comes not from peace, but from an intensified electric energy.

Then I looked down at the locker. I couldn't see what was in there, the thing that had frozen her like that. But I could see the inner side of door. There was a red dot, as if someone had stabbed the door with a marker pen. Except that the ink from a marker pen doesn't drip, and this red dot had two small, dried rivulets running from its bottom edge.

I scanned the area. There were plenty of kids around, but none close enough to see.

She shut the locker.

And for the first time she looked at me. Not so much at me, as at the space I occupied.

"Are you OK?" I asked, not bothering with any of the smiles. If only I'd had one that said, *I know something really, really awful has just happened in your locker, but you can trust me and together we'll get through this.* You'd need some mouth to get that one across.

Her eyes took a while to focus. They were lovely eyes. Here in the shadows they were the colour of the sea on a rainy day.

"You're that kid, aren't you? The one that killed the roaches. The psychopath."

Word travels fast. The worse the word, the faster it goes.

"Stick insects. And, yes, I'm that kid, but, no, I

didn't kill them. I was just *there*."

"And now you're just here." Her face was distant, but desolate, like a wilderness seen from afar. "Did you do this too?"

She sounded almost dreamily calm.

"What's in the locker?"

"Dead stuff."

The idea formed in my head like a figure stepping out of the fog: it was another of the school animals. I knew it the way you know a familiar face in a crowd.

"Let me guess." I made like a chicken, flapping my elbows and doing that chicken thing with my head. I don't know why; it would have been easier just to say "chickens".

She shook her head.

"Guinea pigs?"

She nodded.

"Can I look?"

"I *said* you were a psycho."

She spoke with that same detachment, but she moved away a little and I opened the locker door.

The two guinea pigs were there, side by side. They looked weirdly peaceful. Almost as if they were sleeping. I poked one of them with my finger, half thinking it might open its little black eyes, and the whole thing would turn out to be a joke, that it really was a dot of red marker pen on the door. But Snuffy fell over, and his throat gaped like a second mouth. I didn't need to look to know that Sniffy had suffered the same fate. I swung the door to again.

"Looks like whoever did this sliced them open somewhere else, then came and arranged them like this. There'd be more blood otherwise…"

"What is this, *CSI Hamster*?"

I let that ride. The girl was in shock.

"It also looks like they forced your locker – see these scratches here around the keyhole?"

"Why would someone do that?"

"Like you said, plenty of psychos about."

"I didn't say there were plenty. I said you were one."

"You're pretty cool," I said, "for a girl who's just found two mutilated bodies in her locker."

And then I wished I hadn't said it, because I saw that the stillness I had perceived was an illusion, and that she was trembling. I put my hand on hers. It was as cold as a corpse, and I felt a shiver run through me.

"What's your name?"

"Zofia Novak."

"Cute: a zed name. I like zed names."

For the first time she smiled. It was the briefest smile, like a bird flying across a window.

"And you're…"

"John. Not so cute."

"Let me be the judge of that," she said, and now we were both smiling.

"You're new," I said, in a harmless kind of way.

She gave me a slow, quizzical stare. She really was absurdly beautiful. There was no need for it. She could have shaved the top third off her beauty and still qualified as a goddess.

"There's nothing new under the sun," she said at last. "Don't you realize we've all been here before?"

"We have?"

"The eternal recurrence."

"The what?"

"Eternal recurrence. The universe is big enough and old enough for everything that happens to happen again. And again. And again. Death and rebirth. We're all old news."

Normally that was about the time I'd be laughing or at least walking away, shaking my head.

Except… Recurrence, doubling, rebirth… Somehow it chimed with that feeling I'd had about the two worlds, the one made of light, the other of … whatever it was. As if the recurrence were folded back on itself. Wait, there was a word I remembered, half-remembered … *palimpsest*. Yeah, that was it. Back in the days when they used to write on parchment made from animal skins, they would sometimes scrape off the top layer of writing and start again. But the first layer would never be completely erased and would show through, and so you'd get the two texts almost blending together. Was that why those green eyes haunted me? Had they burned their way through from an older stratum?

Who was I kidding? The reason I didn't walk away was that she was as pretty as a hummingbird chasing a butterfly around a rose.

I tried to think of something witty to say. It was no good; I had nothing in the tank. So I settled for raising an eyebrow, which had gotten me out of plenty of scrapes in the past. She took up the slack.

"But, yeah, new."

"Where were you before?"

"Belmonte."

"Nice school."

Belmonte was an all-girl-private joint. Run by nuns.

"They expelled me."

Well, if she looked like this when she was there, I wasn't surprised that the good sisters kicked her out. But then I remembered something else.

"Wait ... that was *you*?"

"They lied. It was all lies."

"I believe you."

The story had been all over the town. It even made the local paper. A girl, who couldn't be named for legal reasons, had been expelled for practising black magic. It was absurd, of course. There were no details, just gruesome rumours. And now I thought about it, hadn't there been something to do with animals...? Animals being ... *sacrificed*? I felt a twinge of pressure behind my eye. But then I looked again at that lovely face and knew that she was incapable of anything cruel.

"They didn't understand what I was... No, I don't want to talk about it."

It felt as though we'd been standing in a bubble, but suddenly I remembered that there was a real world out there and two dead guinea pigs under our noses.

"Maybe we'd better go and report this," I said, waving my hand at her locker.

"No!" she said in a voice that suddenly burned hot as phosphorous. "They'll say it was me. They'll say it's happening again, they'll say it's because I'm a..."

"You're no witch. Any more than I'm a psycho. OK, then, we need some time to think this over. Lock the door. We can—"

And then I heard something that I should have been expecting, given the way things were going.

"LOCKER INSPECTION!"

CHAPTER TWELVE
AN ACT OF GALLANTRY

A couple of times a term the Shank would prowl down the locker corridor, looking for trouble. He had a master key to all the lockers, but he liked to pick on some poor, furtive, sweating kid, and get him or her to open their own locker. The Shank would almost look disappointed if he didn't find something nasty in there. And if he did find some contraband – a dirty book, maybe, or some of the unhealthy snacks he'd banned from the school – then the victim would get the full blast of his wrath. There was a story that the Shank had once made a kid lick his locker clean when he found it grimed with football-field mud and mouldy cake crumbs.

The Shank was still at the far end of the corridor.

Kids quailed and melted before him, avoiding eye contact, lest he pick on them. He walked on, ignoring them all, his tread heavy and ominous. There were three prefects with him – Funt and Bosola, of course, plus a creepy, lanky kid called Spode. They smacked heads and kicked butts behind the Shank's back.

Then he saw me, and the hard lines of a frown burnt themselves into his forehead. I knew there was more to his presence here than mere coincidence.

"Shut your locker and get behind me," I said to Zofia, hardly moving my lips. Her hands fumbled with the key. She was a tough cookie, but the Shank ate souls. I took the key from her, and she slipped back between me and the lockers, brushing my body and filling my head with her scent.

On marched the Shank. I made myself meet his eye. It was like staring at the sun.

Suddenly, about ten lockers away, he stopped, and turned upon a bird-like creature who was cowering against the yellow metal doors.

"You, girl! Open up."

There was something odd about this. There was no relish or anticipation in the Shank's manner. He was just going through the motions. The girl opened the locker and stood back, but the Shank hardly looked inside.

"Tidy that up," he said with a wave, and on he came.

Behind him, Bosola added a little wave of his own – a backhand slap that knocked the girl against the wall. Spode grinned his creepy grin. When he smiled all you could see was wet gum.

This was no random check. It was obvious that the Shank had been tipped off. It was equally obvious that it was me he was after. Even though I was clean, and there was nothing in my locker, I felt the panic rise in my gorge, like a bad curry. Innocence wasn't always a defence against the Shank.

Then I thought of Zofia. Maybe this wasn't about me. It could be that she had enemies of her own. The Shank hated the goths and the emos. He wasn't the only one. She needed a friend. I had to protect her.

I put my back against the lockers, not even glancing at Zofia, and I believe I may well have started to whistle. I was trying to look like someone who was trying to look innocent. Meaning someone who had something to hide. My thinking was to draw the Shank to my locker and away from Zofia's.

It worked. The Shank walked right up to me. Then he ran his eyes over a printed sheet in his hands. It was a list of names and numbers. He had that grim little executioner's smile on his face. For the first time I noticed that he was a couple of inches shorter than me.

"You," he said. "What a surprise."

"Life's full of them."

"Open up."

"There's n–nothing in there," I said, trying to sound scared.

Funt and Bosola bared their teeth like jackals. They were expecting meat. Spode showed his gums.

"You open that locker this instant, sonny," said the Shank, excitement and rage sizzling on his tongue.

I opened the locker. I made my fingers tremble. I heard Bosola smile, like a snake sliding over a rock.

I stood back and the Shank stooped and rummaged. While he rummaged, Funt and Bosola eyeballed me. Bosola drew his finger silently across his throat. I made an appropriate gesture back.

The Shank stood up. He looked puzzled. He checked his sheet again, and grunted. He didn't even have a go about the mess in my locker.

He backed off a step, and rechecked his sheet. His master key was in his hand. Another locker door swung open.

The Shank made a noise, a sort of a rasp. It might have been a growl. I glanced down obliquely.

I was expecting to see the spot of blood.

What I saw was a photo cut out of some magazine

and tacked to the inside of the door. I did a double take, straight out of a cartoon. It wasn't Zofia's locker he had opened, but number 525.

The Shank knelt and reached into the locker. He pulled out a worn feather boa, a fluffy mohair cardigan, a pair of tap shoes and a big bottle of perfume with a stopper shaped like pouting lips. He held each item up suspiciously, then handed them back to Funt, Bosola and Spode.

Once again he looked perplexed. Whatever he was after – whatever he thought he was going to get – wasn't happening.

"What are you smirking at?" he demanded of me.

"You say smirk; I say smile."

"So what are you smiling about?"

"It's a whole new day, sir, so what's not to smile about?"

The Shank's eye twitched. He moved closer and breathed in my ear.

"Be careful, boy. Be very careful."

Although he said it as a threat, I couldn't help but think that there was also something of a warning in it. A genuine warning.

For the last time, he checked his sheet of paper. I thought he was going to stump off. But then, almost as an afterthought, he hesitated, bent, and stuck his key into another lock. It was number 524.

Zofia's.

I heard – or maybe just felt – her hiss of breath, a sound more of despair than shock. The door swung open and I saw the small red dot with an almost supernatural precision. But the Shank wasn't looking at the door. He barely even looked in the locker. He quickly moved his hand around the inside, like a cheap magician showing there's nothing in the hat. Then he looked at me again with withering contempt and was gone.

Bosola tried to repeat his slapping trick, but I swayed and his palm smacked into the metal locker.

I turned to smile at Zofia, expecting to see a look of astonishment (not to mention gratitude) on her face, but she was gone too, almost as if she'd never been there. She hadn't even thanked me for saving her life.

All that was left was the smell of violets.

Oh, and the two dead guinea pigs in the pockets of my blazer.

CHAPTER THIRTEEN
THE HIT

SO I headed off to my first lesson – PE – with two stiff guinea pigs filling my pockets, and a buzzing crowd of questions in my head. You didn't have to be Stephen Hawking to figure out that the Shank was expecting to find something in my locker. Whichever doofus planted the bodies messed up and put them in 524 instead of 526. But that didn't change the fact that someone was out to frame me. But why? Sure, I wasn't winning any popularity contests, but I couldn't see why I was important enough to merit this level of intrigue, even if the execution had been slapdash. Was this all down to the Shank himself? Or were there other forces moving behind the scenes?

First things first.

I walked around the corridors for a while to make sure no one was trailing me and then dived into the toilets. In good old cubicle three, I crammed the stiffs into my sandwich box, stood on the seat and hid the plastic coffin under the lid in the high cistern. Then I checked my hair in the mirror and made for the gym.

There are worse things than PE, but most kids don't get the opportunity to be buried up to the neck in the desert, their face smeared with honey while ants slowly eat their eyeballs out. It's not even that I don't like sports. It's just that standing in a muddy field while the mentally unstable, and genuinely terrifying, PE teacher Mr Pick screams at you, and a wind like a samurai sword slices into your bare legs, hardly counts as a sport, unless you also reckon that bear-baiting, cockfighting and Russian roulette should be in the Olympics.

But today we had some good news. The steady drizzle had turned into hard rain. That meant indoor games.

As we all filed into the gym, I noticed straight away that Pick wasn't there. You could tell by the eerie absence of screaming. The "we", by the way, was my form class, plus one other. So, 68 kids altogether. That could be a handful. Not a handful for Pick, with whom you messed at your peril. But certainly for Miss Budbe.

Miss Budbe was Pick's second in command, and she was as sweet and sane as he was sour and mad. It was her job to teach the girls about netball, intimate hygiene and socially transmitted diseases. She wasn't like the other teachers. Most of them looked like members of some completely different species of mammal altogether, you know, *Homo educatus*. You looked at the kids, then looked at them, and you just couldn't see how you could make the transition from one to the other.

But with Miss Budbe the connection was there. I'm not saying you'd mistake her for a teenager, but at least she looked like she might actually have been one, and not very long ago. She was as pretty as magnolia flowers before they go brown and turn to sludge on the pavement. One day Miss Budbe would wilt, but for now she was still fresh and pink and fragrant.

Fragrance she had, but not really much in the way of natural authority, by which I mean the ability that some teachers have to make you do what they want by scaring the living *merde* out of you. The couple of times that Miss B. had taken a gym class all on her own, things had pretty quickly descended into chaos.

We sat down on the benches and she started talking. I don't know what she was talking about, because everyone else had begun to talk as well.

Then I heard a voice in my ear:

"Don't turn round."

Of course, someone saying to you, "Don't turn round", is roughly equivalent to them saying, "Turn round or I'll kill you."

So I turned round and looked into the furtive face of Rat Zermatt.

Rat was one of the Bacon-heads. He paid for his dope by thieving, lying, smuggling and snitching. He was forever picking at the scabs around his nose, and like the other 'heads, he was followed wherever he went by a cloud smelling of dead pig and sulphur, like the devil's own barbeque.

"I said don't turn round," he hissed, blowing the smell of old meat into my face. "They'll see me talking to you."

I turned to the front again. I didn't want to spend any more time looking at Rat than I had to.

"Go soak your scabs, Rat."

"I'm trying to do you a favour, schmuck."

"Brushing your teeth is the best favour you could do me. Follow it up with a bath and I'll take you bowling."

Rat made a frustrated chittering sort of a noise, like something mean caught in a cage. "Fine, he doesn't want to know. The Lady said to tell him, but he won't listen. Rat did his job. Rat get paid."

"Stop speaking like Gollum, Rat. Just say what you've got to say." This time I didn't turn round. I'd sooner have picked fleas out of a tramp's vest than look at that face again.

"*Now* he wants to know. But maybe Rat don't want to say. Or maybe he gives Rat a little something as well…"

I looked down. I could see one of Rat's bare, pasty feet. He'd sold his gym shoes for a bag of junk. There was a clump of black hairs on his big toe. I gripped those hairs between my finger and thumb, and yanked. Rat made a gulping screech.

"Talk."

"Please, no… *Ow! Ow! Ow!*"

"Talk."

"The Lady, she give me a message. She said there's a hit. A hit on—"

But that was it. I never got any more. The class was moving. Miss Budbe was shouting, although she had that quality of voice that gets harder to listen to the louder it becomes. I heard "Beanbags" and "Hoops".

I looked at my hand and flicked away the tuft of wiry toe-hairs. Rat was gone, and it seemed that we were about to begin the dreaded indoor games.

The girls were dressed in tight black leotards and unforgiving yellow gym skirts. The boys were wearing purple tops and black shorts. For the next twenty minutes we ran around more or less randomly, sometimes with beanbags on our heads, sometimes without. The hoops made a brief appearance, though I'm not sure to what end, as my mind was occupied with what Rat had said. The questions came at me like the quick-fire round on a game show.

A hit.

On me?

Who was the Lady?

What had she told Rat?

When I resurfaced, things had moved on. It was time for dodge ball. Dodge ball had been imported into the school by Mr Pick, who liked seeing kids get smashed in the face by fast-moving circular objects.

Miss Budbe split us up into two mixed packs of boys and girls, all resplendent in black and purple and gold. I didn't care much for the game, so I took up my position at the end of the line, and got ready to fall in front of some gently arcing ball so I could sit out of the mayhem and dream my dreams.

Then I noticed who was standing opposite me.

Big Donna had the build of a sumo wrestler and the short black hair and small black eyes to go with it. She didn't say much to anyone, but there was a rumour that she had taken part in Gypsy knife-fighting tournaments, and it was a definite fact that she had killed with her bare hands the Rottweiler that ate her Barbie. Personally, I'd always thought that maybe there was a delicate soul inside all that muscle, yearning for a fleeting moment of human contact. But as for actually making that contact, I was happy to leave that up to some other chump.

Now I thought there was something *unhealthy* in the way that Donna was looking at me. She wasn't a person you could read easily, but I sensed that there were seismic events stirring beneath the heavy tectonic plates of her unlovely visage. Like what? Lust? Rage? Irritation?

Miss Budbe blew her whistle and balls started to fly. Tough kids threw hard, aiming to hurt. The face was supposed to be off-limits, but once the dodge ball beast was unleashed, the rules were ignored like a fat girl at the disco. The air was filled first with hurtling projectiles, and then with the cries of the wounded and winded.

Next to me a kid caught one in the crotch and went down like he'd been tasered. I was about to take one safely on the shoulder, when again I caught sight of Donna. There was something odd about the ball she was holding. It was far larger than the typical dodge ball. It wasn't made of orange rubber. It was the dull brown of aged leather. In fact, the leather was so old and worn it almost looked like suede. But that wasn't all. I could tell from the strain on Donna's face that this thing was heavy. She looked like she was carrying a piano.

That could mean only one thing. She was holding the fabled medicine ball. The medicine ball lived in the corner of the gym equipment cupboard and had never been used for anything by anyone. It was just too heavy. It might have been filled with depleted uranium or some such. No one even knew what you were supposed to do with it. Fire it from a cannon was the best guess.

But now it was out in the open, held in the burly arms of Big Donna.

I suppose I knew at some level what was going to happen, but I was caught, mesmerized by the spectacle of Donna raising the great ball above her head, drawing it back, taking aim, hurling. It was a prodigious feat of strength and sent the medicine ball not in a gentle arc, but with Euclidean directness straight at me.

Normally I'm the kind of kid who thinks things through. I have opinions on stuff. Opinions. Ideas. Theories. But all I had time to think now was

BAM!

CHAPTER FOURTEEN
INTERZONE

I opened my eyes to see a ring of gawping faces arranged above me.

"John, are you OK?"

It was Miss Budbe's voice, sweet as angel cake.

I tried to say, "No, actually, I'm not OK. Big Donna just tried to kill me with a medicine ball that weighs as much as a baby elephant, and now my face hurts from where the damn thing slapped into me and the back of my head hurts from where I hit the wooden floor of the gym, and I'm caught up in some kind of massive conspiracy involving the Shank, the Lardies and the Queens, and I'm just the tiniest bit concerned that none of this is really happening and that none of you really exist," but that's the sort of wacky idea that can pass through your head when you've just been knocked out by antique pieces of gym equipment.

What I actually said was more like "Ungth."

There was blood in my mouth. I turned my head and spat it out. That scattered the gawpers.

"You'd better get to the sick bay," said Miss Budbe. "Would you like someone to take you?"

I shook my head.

"I'm fine," I managed to say. "I'll go on my own."

I changed out of my gym gear and went out into the rain. It slapped my fat, injured face like it hated me. If it had had any manners, it would have waited in line for its turn.

I wasn't going to go anywhere near the sick bay. There was a chance that Donna's hit was meant to be just serious enough to get me sent there, and that meant a reception committee would be waiting. Paranoid? You wouldn't think that if you'd had the couple of days I'd had.

It was bad news to get caught wandering around inside the school out of lesson time, but then I wasn't planning on wandering around inside the school.

The Rat had been right about the hit. That meant he knew things. Things I needed to find out. The rodent and I were going to have words. But first I had to do a little prep.

Outside the gym, I headed across the six metres of scruffy grass to the spot where the wire peeled up from the school fence. I scraped myself under and then it was a two-minute stroll to the 7/11.

I grabbed three bags of smoky-bacon-flavoured corn puffs from a rack, and then asked the girl at the checkout for a soft pack of Lucky Strikes. She had yellow hair pulled back from her face and tied into a sort of dense stump on top of her head. She looked tough and bored, but she might have been pretty, once.

"How old are you?" she asked without interest.

"Thirty-nine, tomorrow."

"Happy birthday. You got ID?"

She was flicking through a magazine as she spoke. She had small hands and tiny red nails.

"Sure," I said, and showed her the name tag inside the collar of my school blazer.

I went back into school the way I'd come out. The PE lesson hadn't finished yet, and I tracked along the gym wall, with the bare mud of the playing fields away to my left. Then I looped back around behind the kitchens, hit the next corner, and there, waiting for me, was the black opening of the Interzone. At breaktime the gateway to that Underworld would be busy, but there was no Cerberus on guard now.

I hesitated – you always hesitate before you enter the Interzone, unless you're crazed or depraved, jabbering for a fix. It was strange: the pull and the push of the place almost exactly cancelled each other out.

Almost, but not quite.

As I passed through I could have stretched out my arms and touched the damp walls on either side. It always felt like you were slipping into a different dimension when you entered the Interzone. No, it was something more *organic* than that. It felt like you were being swallowed. You had been on the outside of the beast, and now you were on the inside.

It was quiet, but not dead. I sensed movement, heard muffled groans, saw the orange and blue of a Zippo flame flick on and off, on and off, and then the red glow from a lit tab.

At the far end I could see a line of grey light where the passageway ended. That was at the front of the school, and you couldn't get in or out that way because of the razor wire. The authorities couldn't – or didn't want to – totally suppress the Interzone, but they could at least try to keep it from spilling out where the world might see.

The weird thing is that the light at the end of the Interzone never came any closer, no matter how far in you went. In fact, the whole Interzone seemed to expand with you as you moved, as if somehow you were dissolving the matter of the universe, and creating your own space as you went, like some beetle grub burrowing in rotten wood. Or maybe it was the other way round, and the Interzone was inside us, like a black soul, and it was only in this narrow space that the outside world was shut out enough for us to feel it. And just like any soul, the black soul of the Interzone was infinite.

As my eyes adjusted to the gloom, I saw that there were maybe half a dozen figures in there, slumped against the walls or huddled together. The smells – acrid, meaty, sweet, cloying – curled around me like a decaying cat.

I stepped over legs, found a spot a few metres from the opening, and leant against the wall. I tore open the Strikes and lit one: not because I wanted to smoke, but because it was a way to make sure nobody wondered why I might be here.

I looked up, the way you do when you lean back against a wall and smoke. The Interzone was open to the sky, but no sky showed. Coiling metallic tubes and unfathomable pieces of machinery protruded from the walls, eating the light before it reached ground level.

The light may not have made it, but the rain did. The obstructions merely gathered it into unnaturally large drops, the size of oranges, or channelled it into evil, brown rivulets.

No one spoke. The human shapes on either side of me were lost in the secret labyrinth of their own misery. They appeared as insubstantial as the smoke from my cigarettes, and they seemed almost to flicker back and forth between dimensions, sometimes here, sometimes not.

When the school bell went, it startled me out of my thoughts, the way an alarm clock jerks you out of a disquieting dream. More groans rose up from those around me, and there was a wet sound, like the easing apart of membranes.

It took maybe four minutes after the bell rang for them to arrive. The first were the Bacon-heads, scurrying like vermin. Then, a few thunderous Lardies. Then, more furtively, other figures. Some attenuated and frail, others moving like shadows over the wall. Hiding among them were the predators and parasites that fed on the desperate and the forlorn, bringing junk for the Bacon-heads and pies for the Lardies.

I hung back against the wall and let them all flow or scurry past, although I had that familiar feeling that if I stepped out they'd pass straight through me, like comedy ghosts on TV.

And there, at last, was Rat Zermatt. He took

two, three, four little steps into the Interzone, then he stopped. I heard him sniff the air. His expression changed, and he began to turn. That was when I made my move. I grabbed his collar and threw him against the wall. He clawed at me with his paws, and his little feet kicked out, trying to find a vulnerable spot.

"Who authorized the hit?" I said, trying to keep my voice even.

I wanted Rat to know that I was thinking clearly and not just in some kind of a red rage. The more rational he thought I was, the less likely he was to bullshit me.

He cringed and shook his head and made a high-pitched, inhuman sound.

"Then tell me who sent the warning."

Again he emitted that high, chittering, bat-like noise. I felt my flesh crawl. I wanted to punch Rat more than I'd ever wanted to punch anyone or anything in my life, and I pulled my hand back as he cowered and whimpered.

"Give me a name," I hissed, and my own voice sounded ratlike as well.

Then I felt sick: sick with myself, sick with Rat, sick with the world. I was taking things out on Rat that weren't his fault.

I could do carrot as well as stick. I let him go. He slumped down and then tried to slither away. The scrunch and rustle of the packet brought him back.

"You like?" I said, holding out the bacon-flavoured corn puffs.

Rat released a sound of inchoate yearning, like an orphaned child might make when he sees his dead mother in a dream. He reached for the puffs, slowly, at first, and then with a lightning dart, so quick you couldn't see his hand move. But I was ready for it, and I snatched the prize away.

"Play nice now, Rat, and you'll get what you want."

He writhed and squirmed some more, like a snake under a boot. There was a battle going on inside him, and both sides were fighting dirty.

I opened the packet.

"Speak, or this goes in the gutter."

I began to tilt it.

It was too much for him. He still couldn't speak the words, but he began to scratch something in the filth, using his talons.

I leant over to try to read it – and that's when Rat made his move. He lunged for the puffs, and this time he was too quick for me. He scampered away to what he thought was a safe distance, shoved his paw into the bag he'd stolen and began to shovel the contents into his mouth. After a few pawfuls, he mashed up the bag, grinding what was left of the contents down to a fine powder. He licked his finger, stuck it into the bag, then rubbed the orange mess into his gums, all the time making an urgent, joyless sound. Then, with just a few grains left, he stopped, and carefully tore the bag fully open, like a pathologist opening up a body for an autopsy. He put it on the floor and knelt next to it. Then he took a piece of paper from his pocket – I looked closely and saw it was a pink five-hundred dollar Monopoly note – rolled it tightly, and used it as a tube to snort up what was left in the bag.

I turned back to the message he had scratched on the floor.

The Lardies.

That was all it said. It was enough. So I knew who wanted me out of the way. Now I needed to know why.

I heard a rustle and looked up. Rat Zermatt was gone. But I saw a shape moving in the space between the shadows – a great, brown sewer rat with a tail as thick as a finger. It looked at me, and then re-entered the perpetual murk of the Interzone.

I turned my back on the scene and stalked out of there, my mind full of darkness. Except, that is, for one point of light. The Lardies had authorized the hit, but a girl had sent me a warning, and that girl had to be Zofia. Sure, she owed me, but in this school plenty of debts went unpaid.

CHAPTER FIFTEEN
FORBIDDEN FLESH

THINGS were slightly clearer. But only in the way that the fog lifts just as night is falling.

Big D.'s attack on me and the animal slayings had to be linked, that much I knew. The Lardies were behind the hit. Did that mean that they were also responsible for the killing of the pets? It was the closest thing I had to a lead, and so I was going to pay my respects at the court of King Lard.

But first I had to make another quick visit to my favourite lavatory cubicle, where something was waiting for me with the infinite patience of the dead.

The low-caste Lardies all refuelled down in the Interzone, but the Lardy King and his acolytes had cosier quarters up in the Domestic Science room. The deal was that the kids who were studying catering had to learn to prepare and serve fancy food. The Lardies had the onerous task of eating it.

I knew the kid on the door. Everyone called him Hobnob. I'd stuck up for him once when a couple of scumbags were giving him a hard time back in Year Seven. He'd put on a lot of weight since then. Not all of it was flab. Now he could stick up for himself. But he'd lost something along the way. He used to grin like a child's picture of the sun; now his face was as blank as a pork chop.

He nodded.

"I've come to see the boss," I said.

"Boss eating."

"He's a smart kid; he can do more than one thing at a time."

"Sure can: sausage and egg on the same fork."

"Just tell him I'm here, Hobnob. He'll see me."

"I move from this door and I'm toast. And the boss definitely don't like toast. Not without jam on it."

"Tell him I've got something new."

"New what?"

"New food."

"Ain't no new food. The boss tried it all."

"I haven't got time for this, Hobnob," I said, and

began to squeeze past him through the doorway. Big mistake. He didn't bother trying to hit me. He just eased out his bulk and crushed me against the frame.

One of my rules is never fight a fat guy. There's nothing in it for you. Either you come out of it looking like a bully, or you get sat on, and that's your reputation shot for good.

I tried to free my arms, but Hobnob had me pinned. It was like dancing with an elephant in a broom cupboard. He took hold of my face in his fat fingers.

"Shouldn't have done that, Middleton," he said.

Hobnob's bulk engulfed me, like a white blood cell swallowing a bacterium. I couldn't breathe. I tried to force my knee up into his groin, but it just sank harmlessly into marshmallow.

"Naughty, naughty," he said, and gave me a couple of slaps. Despite the pain and the whole not-being-able-to-breathe thing, my biggest fear was that someone would see all this happening.

"Let him go."

The voice was quiet, hardly more than a wet murmur, like some soft-bodied thing slowly turning in a swamp. But it did the trick. Hobnob inhaled, and I was free, leaving an imprint of my body in his. If you'd had a couple of bucketfuls of hot wax you could have filled it up and sent the results off to Madame Tussauds.

"Your lucky break," I said to the big guy. "I was about to bleed all over your shirt."

"Sure thing, Middleton," he said, but he'd already lost interest.

A long table was set up at the far side of the Dom. Sci. room. There was a fine linen cloth, white as an angel's wing, and the whole table was laid with antique silver, heavy as medieval armour. Six tall, silver candlesticks did a funeral march down the centre. Long-stemmed, white roses were scattered over the cloth like beautiful murder victims. Raised platters overflowed with tumbling bunches of red grapes.

Just one person sat at the table, while others in white jackets fussed around him. Two more heavies stood guard behind. I recognized them as Jethro and Tull.

The "him" was Hercule Paine, the Lardy King.

Hobnob was big, but Paine was bigger. His neat, brown hair sat on top of his head like a tiny plastic hat. Everything beneath it was supersized. His fat face flowed like lava into and beyond his fat neck. Further down, there was a simple, sublime immensity of flesh. He made the two guys behind him look like the testicles on a bulldog.

Which isn't to say Paine didn't dress well. He was definitely a dandy. He wore a silk shirt, and his school blazer had been hand-tailored in a brushed velvet as thick and soft as a seal-pup pelt. There were rings on his fingers and, for all I knew, bells on his toes.

"Nice spread," I said, jerking my thumb at the table.

Hercule Paine looked at me. His eyes were black and unreadable. He moistened his lips with the tip of his tongue, and spoke:

"These" – he waved his hand airily; his fingers were surprisingly long and elegant – "people are preparing for an examination, an HND, I believe, in catering. I, and my associates, assist them, insofar as we can."

I had to strain to catch his words, so faintly did he speak. But, also, I caught a whiff of something foul on his breath; something like rotted meat sweetened with peppermint.

At that moment two white-jacketed flunkies brought in an enormous silver platter. They set it down before the king, and then one of them took off a lid the size of the Millennium Dome. Beneath it was some kind of roast bird. It was so big that, for a second, I thought it might be an ostrich.

Paine exuded an ennui heavy as osmium.

"Swan. Again. Take it away."

"But, sir," said one of the flunkies, almost cringing, "please, wait…" Then he cut into the bronzed flesh with a long carving knife that glinted under the strip lights. "Sir, you see, inside the swan, a goose; inside the goose, a duck; inside the duck, a—"

"Boring."

"But ... but..."

The flunky's hand was resting on the table. Paine, with a speed that belied his bulk, brought his fork fizzing down right between the kid's fingers, jamming it through the white cloth and into the wood beneath. The kid looked down, his face now matching the colour of his jacket and the tablecloth. The fork had nicked the skin of his middle finger, and a drop of blood welled from the cut.

"Go."

The kid scuttled away, holding his hand. The other servant reached for the platter, but Paine dismissed him with a tiny movement of his finger. Then he reached into the huge carcass, rummaged around like a gynaecologist, and emerged with a tiny bird between his finger and thumb. He closed his eyes, opened his mouth, and crunched it, beak, legs and all.

"Lark," he said, his eyes still closed. Then he belched, softly.

I looked at the mess on the table, and for a moment, the fat glistened on the surface and the swan shimmered and became the sweet wrappers and crisp packets and all the other crap that obese kids eat. My mouth was dry and a cement mixer churned in my head.

Paine opened his eyes and turned his attention back to me.

"You look unwell," he said. "Sit, before you swoon into the swan. I don't want to make a mistake and find that I have eaten you too…"

To be honest, I was pretty grateful for the chance to sit. I pulled a chair from the table, and waited.

Paine didn't say anything for a while. He beckoned to one of the heavies and they held a whispered conversation. Then Paine focused back on me and his beady eyes seemed to have, deep within them, a sparkle of green light.

"So, I hear you've had … *difficulties*," the big guy said.

"You hear right."

"And you think that perhaps I have had something to do with these *difficulties*."

"Let's say I've been led to understand that you might be able to help me with a couple of *issues*."

"Issues, issues, always issues. Life should be simple. But always issues."

"Yeah, well, my issue is that I just got a medicine ball in the face."

"I'm sorry to hear that."

"Maybe you are. And maybe you're not. Either way, it was your girl, Big D., who propelled it. And I know she's just a dancing bear, and it's you who's blowing the bagpipes."

"It seems that someone has a big mouth."

Paine's eyes drifted off into the distance, and I suddenly felt a twinge of guilt about Rat. I didn't like the rodent, but I also didn't want him stinking up my conscience like cat shit behind the curtains.

"Or maybe I've got big ears. It didn't take a lot to figure it out."

"Well, then, let us assume that your deduction is correct – purely for the sake of argument, of course. You understand that I run an organization – one that the hoi polloi term, impertinently, the Lardies."

"Yeah, sure. You smuggle in junk food for you and the other fat kids. Big deal. And just so we're clear, when I say 'big deal', I'm being sarcastic. What I mean is a deal so small you could fit it on a Ritz cracker."

One of the heavies behind Paine growled and took a step towards me. The boss stopped him with a murmured, "Not now, Jethro. Play later."

"You disgust me, Paine," I said, not loudly, but clearly. Maybe I was trying to kick things off. I reckoned I could do some damage to Jethro and Tull, maybe even the boss himself, before they took me out. But Paine wasn't easily riled.

"I provide a service. It's simple economics. There is a need. I meet it. Hunger is a wolf that, in the absence of meatier sustenance, devours the soul. I feed the wolf, and save the soul."

"Fascinating stuff. As an excuse for making serious money out of bun-running it takes some beating. But I know you're cheek by jowl with the prefects in this. And anyone who lies down with a donkey wakes up smelling of ass."

"Then you would know also that I have to tread more carefully than I might otherwise desire. My operations are intricate and delicate as a cobweb. There are connections, lines, patterns. There are powers stronger than my little operation. Powers that must be … *appeased*."

"So, you're just the sub-contractor," I said. "Who's the main guy? Who's pushing the buttons?"

Paine shrugged. He could shrug just using his fat face.

"Were you not listening? I cannot tell you without jeopardizing everything I have built."

I picked at a nail. "You don't think I could cut a few of those silken lines?"

"I dare say you could cause a little damage. Before you were crushed. I promise you, this is a fight you cannot win. There is a hierarchy of power, a pyramid, and you are part of the base."

Paine was a crook, but that didn't mean he wasn't deep. He was right about the power. But I wasn't here to threaten. I was here to buy.

"You hungry?" I asked.

"The wolf never slumbers for long. The problem, of course, is novelty. There is so little left that I haven't tried."

"I think I may have something that could help you with that. Something ... *new*."

I had his attention.

"And you think to barter with me?"

"You're a businessman. Let's do some business."

"Might I ask to see your ... currency?"

I reached a hand into each blazer pocket. The heavies behind Paine sprang forward, like spooked hippos.

"Take it easy!" I said, and slowly drew out the two guinea pigs. "Forbidden flesh. Is anything sweeter?"

I put the two corpses on the tablecloth. The table now looked like a seventeenth-century Dutch still life.

"Do I see before me the school guinea pigs? Snuffy and...?"

"Sniffy."

"Of course I'd heard on the grapevine that ... well,

so it's true, you are the killer. Now it falls into place. I quite see why he … why it was thought desirable to have you eliminated. Funny, even though we all knew about your past … *troubles*, I'd never have guessed you had something like this in you."

"You've no idea what I've got in me. But that doesn't mean I killed these guys."

Paine raised a sceptical eyebrow. I didn't press the point any further. It might be useful to be mistaken for a rodent-slaying maniac.

"Ever eaten guinea pig?" I asked.

"No. But I am, naturally, aware that in parts of South America they are considered to be a delicacy."

He couldn't keep his eyes off the bodies. His upper lip was beaded with moisture. He had started to breathe more heavily.

"A name. Give me a name. That's all I want, and then they're yours any way you want them. Grilled, kebabed, guinea-pig sushi, whatever."

Paine's eyes darted back and forth between the meat and me. Then, suddenly, he clapped his hands. Instantly, the white-jacketed lackey he had pronged with his fork reappeared.

"Take these to the chef. Have them skinned and gutted. This one here, I want raw and finely sliced, carpaccio style, dressed in olive oil and a little lemon juice and basil. The other, I want roasted with fennel and sweet potatoes. And tell Chef to keep the heads for stock."

The lackey reached for the guinea pigs. I grabbed his arm, and looked at the boss.

"That name."

Paine hesitated, licked his lips, and then said, "The Dwarf."

CHAPTER SIXTEEN
BACK TO THE SHANK

THE Dwarf. Why did it have to be the Dwarf?

I squeezed out of the room, past Hobnob, with the words pinging and echoing in my head like a cry of pain in an underpass. I'd asked for a candle and been handed a stick of dynamite.

Did Paine mean that the Dwarf was the killer? Or just that he had answers, that he was another of the arrows leading me to the end. To my end...

The Dwarf had lurked in the collective unconscious of the school for a long time. He was the spectre haunting our half-forgotten memories and dreams. And like all the ghouls and terrors of the unconscious, he was there because we'd repressed him. Well, I was going to have to un-repress him. I was the scared child who would have to climb out from the protecting bed covers and confront the beast in the wardrobe. I shivered at the thought.

But not for long, because a new problem presented itself. Presented itself in the sense of grabbing me around the neck and throwing me down on the hard floor.

Funt and Bosola. Waiting for me out in the corridor.

"Hello, scrote-head," said Bosola. "You are in some serious, serious shtick now."

"Do you even know what shtick means?" I asked, looking up his nose from my position on the floor.

"Well it ain't good," he sneered. "And, like I said, you're in it."

And then he did something unexpected. Given how predictable he was, you really didn't expect the unexpected from Bosola. What he did was to levitate. Funt joined him, six inches off the floor. Neat trick, I thought, even if they had a little help. The help was supplied by Hobnob, who had a collar in each hand. He was a slick mover for a big guy, and had materialized soundlessly behind the two thugs.

"Get off, you fat fruit," yelped Bosola. "This is Shank business."

Hobnob banged their heads together in a friendly sort of a way. "If I put you down, you play nice. Johnny's a friend of mine."

Then he dropped them.

All three of us got off the floor together.

"Thanks, Hob," I said.

"Old times' sake. And remember," he added, looking at Bosola and Funt, "play nice." Then he turned to me again. "One more thing, Middleton…"

"Yeah?"

"The Dwarf."

"Yeah?"

"Don't."

"Why?"

"It's a trick. The Dwarf, he'll—"

"I've no choice. Either I find out who's behind all this or I'm finished."

Hobnob stared at me. His face was a blank canvas showing no emotion, which made it tempting to paint something on there. Pity? Sympathy? Understanding? Or, like everyone else, did he just think I was a psycho?

"In that case," he said finally, "you'll need to know something."

"What?"

"His real name. It might just save you."

Then he whispered the name in my ear.

"OK, you two fairies," said Bosola, "enough of the heavy petting. Let's go before the blimp gets himself a puncture."

He patted the inside pocket of his blazer. The suggestion was plain enough. Hobnob stared him down.

"It's cool, Hob," I said, and began walking all by myself towards the Shank's office. After a second or so the prefects followed.

"Hey, wait for us," said Funt. "We was told to drag you. We're supposed to… I mean you aren't meant to—"

"Shut up," said Bosola.

They were still scuttling behind me when I reached the Shank's office. I knocked and went straight in. Bosola followed right behind, and made a point of grabbing me, so we half fell through the doorway together.

"Got him, like you asked, Chief," Bosola panted. "I—"

"How dare you burst in here like this," said the Shank, hurriedly putting something away in his desk. It might have been a bottle.

"But he … but I…"

"Just get out. No, not you, Middleton. You stay right where you are."

The Shank contemplated me like a vivisectionist. The malice flowed out of him like dry ice from a beaker in the chemistry lab, and something inside me seriously considered shivering.

Then it began:

"Where are they, Middleton?"

"What? The treasures of El Dorado? The hopes and dreams of your youth? The heroes of yesteryear? Your car keys? I give up. Try the Internet."

"You know very well what I mean. The guinea pigs – where are they?"

"Not in their cage? Don't tell me they tunnelled out? Well on their way to Switzerland now, I should guess, if their papers are in order."

"I'm going to try one more time. If I get a similarly flippant answer, you are going to spend an hour in the sick bay with our friends Funt and Bosola, ably supported by as many other prefects as it takes to make sure that you are ... *comfortable*. Do I make myself clear?"

"As the Pope's conscience."

"So, where are the guinea pigs?"

"I have no idea."

It's always easier to lie when you're telling the truth. I genuinely didn't know which part of Paine's digestive tract Sniffy and Snuffy would have reached by now. Stomach? Small intestine? Large intestine? Who could say?

The Shank drilled a hole in my skull and had a quick look around. Then he glanced down at the papers on his desk.

"This morning I received a note suggesting that I would find something interesting in a certain locker. When I went to check, I found you adjacent to the locker in question, with a look on your face that exceeded even your generally high background level of guilt. Shortly afterwards, I was informed that the school guinea pigs were not in their cage. Despite your well-known *problems*, Middleton, I am told that you are not a stupid boy. So why don't you use that brain of yours and tell me what deductions *you* would draw from those facts?"

It was my turn to pause. I tried to get everything straight, but the inside of my head was like a washing machine, with the animals, the people, the places churning in a mush of grey suds. By a huge effort of will, I made it stop, and sorted through the laundry.

"I'd say it was a set-up. Whoever nabbed the pigs tried to plant them on some patsy. A patsy with the initials J. M. But either they were too dumb to get it right, or the guys they put on the job were too dumb."

"And why would anyone want to implicate you in this? You don't think that smacks of paranoia?" The Shank's tone softened a little and he added, "We've been here before, John."

"Sure. The eternal recurrence."

"What?"

"Oh, nothing. Just something someone said... But it's not paranoia when they're really trying to get you."

Again the Shank bored into me. Again he found nothing but an empty space.

"I don't know exactly what's going on here, Middleton, but I know you're at the heart of it. Turn your pockets out."

"What, you think I'd be walking about with dead guinea pigs in my pockets?"

"Just do what I say."

I flapped and slapped, showing the Shank I was clean. He didn't notice the couple of white hairs that fluttered down to the carpet.

"Proves nothing," he said. "You could have dumped the bodies anywhere."

"That would be the smart move."

The Shank rubbed his eyes with the heels of his hands. He looked and sounded tired.

"Today is Wednesday. At 12 p.m. on Friday I will be holding an all-school assembly. If this situation has been cleared up by then, the purpose of the assembly will be to wish the Drama Club the very best of luck with the performances of *The Wizard of Oz*. If no resolution has occurred, then the school will hear that the performances, scheduled for the following Friday and Saturday nights, have been cancelled because of you. I derive no pleasure, no pleasure whatsoever, from this."

"I bet," I said.

"What's that supposed to mean?"

"It's supposed to mean that something stinks here. There's something corrupt and rotten, and the rottenness goes down to the core."

"Get out of here, Middleton."

"I'm gone."

As I was leaving I heard what sounded like a click. It was the Shank's brain changing gear.

"Wait, dead. You said 'dead'. How do you know the guinea pigs are dead?"

For once I was stumped. I cursed myself for being such a dumb-ass.

"Just a guess. Based on the pattern."

"The pattern?"

"Yeah, you know, like the picture of the skull on a death's-head moth. The pattern of stuff dying."

And I got out of there while that one was still rolling around in his cerebral cortex.

At the end of the staff corridor, I almost bumped into Hart. My head was still back in the Shank's office, or I'd have checked out where he was going. As it was, we both raised our chins in greeting, and then I was lost in the churning humanity of the school, as one lesson ended and the next began.

I know I should have tried to make my move on the Dwarf, but somehow the rest of the day contracted into a point, consumed itself, vanished. My mind was a black hole sucking in everything, matter, light, even time.

Things only snapped back into focus as I trudged out of school that afternoon. Every kid was being frisked at the gates. When I was through, I looked back to see Paine getting patted down by a nervous prefect. He beamed beatifically at me, gave a little tinkling wave like Oliver Hardy, then put his hand to his mouth, as if he'd just let slip an accidental burp.

A guinea-pig-flavoured burp.

CHAPTER SEVENTEEN
Some Advice From the Cat

THE house was still empty. I checked the phone for messages. Just one. I hit play.

"Meds!"

That was it. Nothing more. My mum's voice had an edge of hysteria. Nothing new there. Crazy school, crazy home. I was the sane centre of a mad world.

I picked up the dispenser from the top of the fridge and gave it a rattle. I was two days behind now. I couldn't remember if I was supposed to take all the ones I'd missed. Or would that OD me? I could call my shrink... But the thing is, I felt good. Well, OK, not *that* good, but not crazy. The shrink had said that sometimes it's a one-off, what happened to me. Sometimes... Anyway, taking pills when you don't need them, that has to be nuts, doesn't it?

I went to the bathroom and stared at my face in the mirror. There were black smudges under my eyes, but apart from that my face was as colourless as a meal of boiled fish in white sauce.

Tough day.

I went into my room and fell onto the bed. I didn't even take my shoes off. There was something nagging at the outer rim of my consciousness. Something I was supposed to do. Or not do. The Dwarf. My pills. Other things. I rested my eyes for a few seconds. When I opened them again, two hours had slipped by. I had a taste like burnt hair in my mouth and the feeling that someone had taken out my brain and replaced it with scrunched-up aluminium foil.

I brushed my teeth and then went down to the kitchen and ate a can of peaches. That helped. It always helps. The house was eerily quiet. It was something more than just the absence of noise. The silence felt like an actual presence, something that had flowed like an inert gas into the rooms. The thought of the stifling gas made my throat tighten, and I knew that there was only one place to go.

Up on the roof, I waited for Cat to come.

I knew she would.

"*Grrrrrrrrrrrrrrmmmmmmmmmmm,*" she said.

I opened the sardines. She poked her nose quickly in and out.

"Not hungry tonight?"

"Already ate. Been checking out the neighbourhood. That old lady at number 14…"

"You ate the old lady?"

"Funny."

"I work at it."

Of course I knew that cats couldn't really talk, and that I was imagining words in the random cat noises that she made, but her voice made me feel better, somehow. I guess I was missing my family.

"So, tell me, how are things at school?" she asked.

"You don't want to know."

"You can't tell a cat what it wants."

She jumped onto my lap. It made me start. I looked down. It was a long way.

"School's fine. Struggling a bit with maths and physics, sailing through English lit and history."

"Yeah, like *that's* what I meant."

"OK then. You asked for it. There's trouble. Some sicko is bumping off the school pets. I've been on the scene once too often, so the Shank – that's the Deputy Head – has me down as a suspect. But the Principal – Mr Vole – well, he's three-quarters senile, but he's basically OK, and he's got me trying to figure out who's behind it all. But things are getting murkier. Someone's trying to frame me. Or maybe just scare me off. Or perhaps just mess with my head. I don't know. And then there are the Queens—"

"The *what*?"

"The Drama Queens – you know, the theatre club."

"OK."

"Well, they're mixed up in this, and the Queen Mum – don't ask – well, she's on my back as well. And when I went to the Lardies to try to find out who had hired Big Donna to sing me to sleep, all I got was a faceful of hot flab and a ticket to go visit the Dwarf."

"Dwarf?"

"That's what we call the school caretaker. Evil little dude lives in the Underworld."

"The Underworld…? This dwarf lives in Hell?"

"It's a figure of speech. The Underworld is the basement area beneath the Interzone. The ass-end of the ass."

The cat snickered. Couldn't tell if she was laughing *with* or laughing *at*.

"I see now why you look tired. Any good news?"

"Well, someone's trying to help me. There's a girl—"

"I thought so. There's always a girl."

"Zofia."

"Hey, a zed name. I like a zed name."

"Funny, that's just what *I* said. Well, I helped her out when those two stiff guinea pigs showed up in her locker... OK, I see I'm losing you here, Cat."

"It is all a bit far-fetched. I guess you've got a lively imagination."

I grunted and pulled the crumpled Warrant out of my trouser pocket. "What about this, then?"

"Means nothing to me. I can't read. Oh, do you hear that?"

"What?"

"Phone. Better answer it."

"It's only Mum."

"Not this time, I don't think."

"Psychic?"

"Feline intuition. Go, tiger."

Then the cat leapt up and over the roof like Spring-heeled Jack, and I scrambled for the phone.

CHAPTER EIGHTEEN
STARBUCKS

HER: "Hi."

It took me a couple of seconds to place the voice.

Me: "Hi."

Her: "You take some tracking down."

Me: "You're quite the sleuth. How did you…?"

Her: "I'd rather not reveal my methods. A girl needs a little mystery."

Me: "I suppose I should thank you for—"

Her: "Thank me? I don't get it. No, I called to see if … well, do you ever go out?"

Me: "Under cover of dark. Sometimes."

Her: "I thought maybe I could buy you a coffee…"

Me: "Well, maybe you can."

Her: "And maybe you could also tell me what the hell's going on."

Me: "I'll tell you what I know, but the truth is that it doesn't add up to much."

Her: "That'll do. Starbucks?"

Me: "Sure."

Her: "Eight – is that enough time to switch to your night plumage?"

Me: "Eight's good."

Click.

I had a grin on my face, and a date with a zed name.

At one minute to eight I pushed through the door of the Starbucks on the high street.

With a little choke, I saw that Zofia was already at the glass counter. She looked like a black flamingo. She was wearing a long skirt, the colour of night, and a tight jacket with something lacy happening at the wrists and neck. Very Morticia Addams. In a good way.

I walked over and rested my hand lightly on her back. She turned and smiled and I felt that short, sharp punch in the guts that beauty gives you sometimes by way of "hello". Her skin was pale and perfect and covered, as far as I could tell, the whole of her body.

"Sorry if I kept you waiting."

"I just arrived."

I bought her a coffee – she wanted some weird mix with cinnamon and vanilla. I ordered mine black. I hate black coffee, but I thought it might impress her.

I led Zofia over to a quiet booth against the wall. The place was dotted with idlers reading newspapers or gazing into space, which meant that there wasn't quite enough of a buzz to disguise the slightly embarrassing silence when we sat down.

It was Zofia who filled it.

"You sounded surprised when I called."

"Yeah, well, it was. A surprise, I mean."

"A nice one?"

"Four-balls-in-the-lottery nice."

I threw her my second-best smile. I wanted to keep something in reserve for emergencies.

"I just wanted to say … what you did … at the lockers. It was cool."

"I'm a cool kid," I said, and crossed my eyes and did something stupid with my mouth.

It made her laugh. Suddenly we were having fun. And we carried on having fun while we sipped our drinks. I couldn't remember the last time I'd had a normal, light-hearted, jokey, flirty conversation like this. Zofia may have looked like gloom come to life, but soon those purple lips of hers went up through the gears from pout to smile to grin.

But there were things that needed to be said, on both sides. And so I asked Zofia about her old school, and what had happened there.

She stared into her cup for a while and I thought I'd blown it. Then she spoke:

"It was just… It was nothing. Look, there was this teacher there. Mr Cram. He was weird, you know…?"

"Not really."

"With girls. He used to stand too close to you. And there was something about the way he looked at you…"

"OK, weird like *that*."

"He didn't touch us, but he was still creepy. And then he had a stroke and died."

"Whoa!"

"And then one of the teachers found a little model made out of clay in my desk."

"So what?"

"In the shape of a man."

"Oh."

"There were pins stuck in it."

"Voodoo?"

She shrugged.

"Someone … planted it?" I said, wanting to sound like I was on her side. Hell, I was on her side.

There was a pause and then she nodded. She gazed at the floor with those green, catlike eyes of hers.

"I guess, yeah. Someone's idea of a joke."

"But you got chucked out?"

"I wasn't formally expelled, but it was obvious I couldn't stay there any longer. Not when the papers got hold of it."

Then it was her turn.

"So, that's me and my troubles. I hear you've had you own."

"Yeah. Maybe I should have changed schools too."

Most of the kids knew that I'd had what was described as an "episode". I tried to find the right way to put it.

"I'm not a psycho, if that's what you're thinking."

"I wasn't thinking anything."

"It was just..." What the hell was it? "It was a year ago. I got stressed out by stuff at home. My mum and dad were arguing a lot. And I ... I saw things that weren't really there. No, not quite that. I started to see things that were there in a different way. Or something like that. I started to see *meanings* in ordinary stuff."

"Like what?" Zofia sounded interested. If she was freaked by the whole thing she was doing a good job of hiding it.

"Oh, I don't know. The angle of my desk or the way

a leaf was blowing down the street. It'd be like it was all a *message*."

"Sounds kind of cool."

I laughed. "Yeah, well, I suppose it made each day into a sort of adventure. But then it stopped being fun, and I couldn't leave my room because of all the crap in my head. That's when my mum and dad got me to the shrink."

"And he fixed you up?"

"It was a she. But, yeah, I guess. Well, she gave me some drugs. Strong drugs. And the world stopped talking to me the way it had."

"You almost sound as if you miss it."

I shrugged. Then there was another silence, and I slurped the last of my coffee.

"I suppose," said Zofia, her voice quietly caressing, "all this … stuff that's going on now must … be hard for you?"

"Tougher on the stick insects and the guinea pigs."

"So what the hell *is* going on?"

"You want the facts or my interpretation?"

"Both."

"Right, all we know for certain is that someone killed the sticks – probably poisoning them with ethyl acetate—"

"Nail varnish remover?"

"That's the stuff. Then they – and I've got to assume it's the same guy or guys – sliced up the guinea pigs."

"But why?"

"That's where the water gets muddy. As everyone knows, I got sucked into this because I was on the scene. Now I'm expected to sort it out. It's my only chance of clearing my name. And if I flunk it, then the school play gets cancelled, and I'm going to end up dangling from a lamppost with a feather boa around my neck. And when they cut me down I'll be expelled. The way I figure it, whoever's behind this has a pretty neat twin-pronged manoeuvre going on. They want to break the Queens, which I'm guessing is the first objective, and they want to make it look like it's me that's responsible."

"And you've got someone in mind? I mean the evil genius behind all this?"

"There's only one man who has the right combination of cunning and power. The Sh—"

"Don't say it," she said, and suddenly she looked desolate, like the last flower in a muddy field.

"But why...?"

And I looked at her, at her downcast green eyes that were bright now with tears.

"He's my father."

"WHAT?"

"Shankley. He's my father."

"But you're called…"

"Novak. My mother's name. They are divorced."

"So that's why you disappeared at the lockers."

There were black lines on her cheeks. I felt as numb as a novocained mouth.

The green eyes.

I should have known.

"I'll get a napkin from the counter," I said, meaning to use the few seconds it would take me as quality thinking time.

When I came back she was gone. She hadn't touched her coffee. A man in another booth was staring at me. He was wearing a green hat.

"Did you see where my friend went?" I asked, but he just buried himself in his coat, and pulled the hat down over his face.

"Your hat sucks," I said as I left.

I walked home the long way, which took me down past the school. I was trying to fit the new information into the pattern. But that was the problem. There was no pattern. There was only white noise.

And the Dwarf.

But I didn't want to think about the Dwarf now, so I focused back on the girl. Zofia was the Shank's daughter. Stated plainly like that it seemed insane. How could something so ugly produce something so beautiful? Ugly in spirit, I mean, although even physically the Shank wasn't going to get a contract as an underwear model. The whole thing was yet another layer of complication slapped on top of what was already a head-banger. It was as if someone had hidden a Rubik's Cube inside a massively knotted ball of string.

I tried to unknot the string. The key (and yeah, I know, keys don't help you much with string) was our old friend coincidence. The Zofia–Shank–guinea pig nexus was just coincidence. Had to be. Someone had tried to implicate me, and, by pure chance, they'd stashed the bodies in Shank's daughter's locker by mistake. And even the fact that the Shank and Zofia were related – did that have to signify anything? We'd heard the rumours that the Shank had been divorced. And I supposed that once Zofia was kicked out of the convent she didn't have much of a choice about where she'd go. But it must have been tough. Tough in all kinds of ways.

By the time I reached home my head was throbbing like a stubbed toe. I swallowed four aspirin, gagging on the chalky sourness. There was no sign of the cat. No sign of life at all. I went to bed and dreamed of nothing, for ever.

DAY THREE

THURSDAY

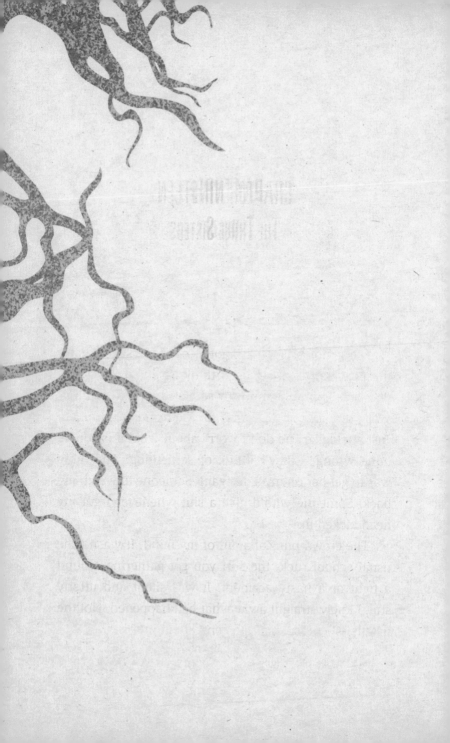

CHAPTER NINETEEN
The Three Sisters

I saw the mob as soon as I got through the school gates the next morning. I'd been thinking about Zofia. My plan was to find her and say sorry. Say sorry for what? Well, the rule is the same for God and for women. Just apologize and don't worry about what it is you've done wrong – they'll think of something. The thing was to get her on my side again. Someone to watch my back. Someone who'd give a shit whenever I got my head kicked in.

The crowd put Zofia out of my mind. It wasn't the usual school ruck, the sort you get gathering around a fight or a nasty accident. It was silent and utterly still. I knew straight away what had happened. Not the details, of course, just the general outline.

It was the chickens.

I pushed my way to the front. I was too late for the first screams, and all that remained of the crowd's emotion was the stunned fascination elicited by violent death.

The chickens – three pale-grey spinsters from the same brood – lived in a wood-framed wire cage, with a cosy, straw-packed wooden box at one end. The names "Olga", "Maria" and "Irina" were written in white paint on the outside of the box. Some said that Olga was sensible and serious, that Maria was witty and vivacious and that Irina was rather silly and romantic, but to me they were just chickens, and I couldn't tell them apart.

The only way into the cage was through the hinged roof, which was secured with a serious padlock. Well, that was the theory.

I peered through the wire. Blood and feathers and unidentifiable gobbets of flesh were smeared, scattered, sprayed all over the run. There was nothing left that looked remotely like a chicken. Except for a beak. A solitary beak, attached to nothing beyond its own symbolism. I also saw that a ten-centimetre square had been cut through the wire.

I closed my eyes and *saw* it happen. The early hours of the morning. A figure, dressed all in black, stealthy, furtive, unhurried yet urgent. The harsh *snick, snick, snick* of the wire cutters. The three sisters clucking nervously, edging back into the warmth of the straw. The dark figure finishes his work and slips silently away. The chickens emerge to sniff at the gap in the wire. Freedom beckons, but freedom to some is more terrifying than captivity, and the three sisters return to the familiar enclosure at the end of the run. And so, twenty minutes later, when the old dog fox comes padding along on his nightly rounds, he finds his supper as neatly packaged for him as a microwave pizza. In a few seconds of efficient butchery, the chickens are dead and dismembered.

"Why? Why? Why?"

I recognized the sad tones of Mr Vole and opened my eyes. I turned to see his bleak, grey face. He was speaking, it seemed, to himself.

"I told them. Bring them in. Bring them in. I sent a memo. They were not safe."

Desolate though he sounded, it was the first time I'd heard the Principal speak without every other word being an "er" or an "ah".

He looked at me. Recognition flickered, but then the flame went out. The kids in the crowd saw me, realized who I was, and a space opened up around me.

"Him," said someone.

"Murderer," hissed another.

"The mental kid."

I saw teeth bared. I saw eyes filled with hate and vengeance. I felt spittle slap into my face. I felt the crunch of fist and foot.

I managed to spin and tear myself out of the hands that grasped, but it was Vole who saved me. He put his arms around me and dragged me out of the mêlée. At first, the kids, half-blinded with rage, didn't heed the fact that it was the Principal who was protecting me, and carried on trying to land kicks and punches. But then other teachers arrived, along with a gang of prefects, and the crowd split up into smaller knots and solitary snarlers. They left, looking over their shoulders like a clan of hyenas driven off a kill by lions.

"Better get to your, er, ah," said Vole.

It was good advice. I scampered with all the dignity of Rat Zermatt to my form room.

Out of the frying pan and into the scorching *merde*. As soon as I entered the form room, I knew things were going to get dirty. Pretty-boy Wilson, my official class tormentor, was waiting for me. He and three or four other boys were sitting on the desks at the front of the room. As I came through the door, he nodded, and I noticed someone slip out behind me.

"Psycho's here," Wilson said, in a whining, psycho voice. The faces around him were hard and fierce.

"Get screwed, Wilson."

I wasn't in the mood for a fight, and I tried to reach my desk. Suddenly the boys were standing in my way.

"You've gone too far this time, nutter," Wilson said. "No one cared about the stick insects and the guinea pigs, but you shouldn't have killed the chickens. They belonged to all of us. You're a mental case and a murderer, and we don't want you here."

I looked behind the mob, trying to find a friendly face. But even the girls stared at me with hatred, and the only thing that diluted the hatred was fear.

"No one's gonna help you, loser. You've no friends here. You've never had any friends here. You're on your own."

That hurt. It hurt because it was true. I had always been on my own.

"The teacher…" I began, but then stopped. It sounded lamer than a three-legged dog.

"Won't help you. Mr Vass is going to be a bit late today."

I thought about the kid that had left as I came in. I imagined him talking to Vass, using some ruse to keep him away. It wouldn't be hard. Mr Vass was a good guy, and he'd looked after me as much as he could, but he would sometimes get distracted by a pattern in the carpet or a shadow on a wall.

"You know I had nothing to do with—"

I never finished the sentence. Someone punched the side of my face. It was a flapping, soft sort of punch, but I didn't see it coming, and it's always the one you don't see coming that puts you on your knees.

I looked up. The faces were blurred. I knew why, and what it signified.

"Hey, look, the psycho's crying," said someone, not Wilson.

Wilson leered at me.

"Not so tough, eh, Middleton? Not unless you're killing little insects and chickens."

"What do you want?" I asked, feeling defeat on me, like skunk spray.

Wilson put on a face that parodied concern.

"We just want you to go." He flicked his hand back towards the door. "Get out of this school and don't come back."

I got up and staggered towards the door. Snot was running out of my nose. I was a cur running with my tail between my legs. But I could still bite. I looked at Wilson, looked at them all. "You're going to look back on what you did here. You're going to remember it. And you're going to beg me for mercy. Beg me on your knees."

As I left I heard a huge sarcastic wail come up from the class, followed by guffaws and apelike laughter.

On the way out I bumped into Mr Vass and the sneak who'd been sent out to delay him. I careened into the wall and ran on. Vass was too surprised even to yell after me.

CHAPTER TWENTY
THE DWARF'S STORY

I'D reached the lowest point. That sorry excuse for a punch had made me weep. And then I'd uttered a threat so feeble it wouldn't have scared a nervous rabbit.

I crashed through the front doors of the school and stood out in the grey light. The rain had come on again, but I welcomed it on my face, where it washed away the tears and the snot, and brought me back to myself. I was in trouble. Serious trouble. It wasn't just the Lardies and the Queens who were on my back now, but the whole school. The only way to save myself was to find the real killer. And I had one clue.

Our school caretaker, the Dwarf.

The story went something like this. The Dwarf had been a pupil at the school back when many of the parents of the current generation were there, and the tale had been passed on down to us, warped, perhaps, by the tricks of memory and the usual lies and exaggerations that creep into all stories, but true in its essentials.

The Dwarf was always a tiny creature: frail, crook-backed – even his face was contorted, as if invisible hands around his forehead and chin were twisting or wringing him out. Looking like that in a school like this was bad news for the kid. He was quick, so he could usually escape the big predators, but there were bound to be times when they caught him, and then a good old-fashioned goading would take place.

So things were always tough for him. But then he made a mistake, and things got a whole lot worse. His mistake – isn't it *always* the mistake – was to fall in love. The girl he fell for was called Galadriel Curtain, and she belonged to another. That might not have mattered so much if the other hadn't been Jud Fray. Fray was blond-haired and blue-eyed enough for any girl, and even his muscles had muscles. He was also a bad kid. You'd have called him evil, except that evil requires a rudimentary intelligence, and Fray was a bare evolutionary notch up from the gibbon. He was the kind of dullard whose mother had to write *This is you* in crayon on the bathroom mirror to stop him from punching it.

Now the thing about the Dwarf is that a silken poet's tongue lurked inside his twisted mouth. From a distance he spied the fair Galadriel, and fell in love up to his armpits. Naturally, Galadriel didn't think much of being courted by a creature that looked like it had just climbed off a church roof. But he plied her with sweet words and soft endearments and stolen gifts. He made her feel in turn as though she were an enchantress in a fable, a fair maid in a tale of knights and dragons, a witty Shakespearean heroine (although, of course, all the wit was his). And finally Galadriel overcame her revulsion, closed her eyes and, concealed from the world by the huge metal bins outside the school kitchens, submitted to a kiss.

It was one moment of pure joy for both of them. In that instant, the Dwarf's soul showed itself to be as straight and true as his body was misshapen. And Galadriel was transformed by that kiss from a pretty, superficial confection of perfume and glitter truly into an enchantress, a fair maid, a heroine.

For seven seconds.

And then the Dwarf was lifted bodily from his rapture and shaken like a rat in the jaws of a terrier.

For the ill-matched lovers had been spied, and the vengeful Fray informed.

The Dwarf opened his eyes to see not just Jud, but

a mocking crowd of his followers and sycophants.

Then Jud slapped Galadriel so hard she fell to the ground. She looked at the hard eyes all around her, and said the words that damned the Dwarf:

"He made me."

For once, the eloquent boy had no words. He lowered his eyes and let them beat him. Would denial have helped him, or would the myth of beauty defiled by the beast have been too strong?

When the beating was done, the torment began. Jud's mind was slow in most ways, but ingenious in the devising of tortures. He had one of the big bins emptied of all but the age-old slime and foul juices at the bottom, and the Dwarf was thrown in. Then what was by now virtually the whole school began to pound on the metal, some with fists, some with improvised clubs (fence posts, cricket bats, unfortunate younger kids), ringing it like a great bell. And as they drummed, they chanted. Not some clever or witty rhyme, but simply one word, repeated over and over again:

Dwarf

    Dwarf

        Dwarf

            Dwarf.

All day they drummed. To begin with he cried out,

begging for mercy. Then his voice became shrill. And then faint, inaudible beneath the clanging. Finally, silence.

One by one the tormentors drifted away, until at last only Jud remained, still beating at the metal with a broken shovel. And then even he grew tired of the sport and left. All was quiet for a minute, for two. Then a figure emerged from the shadows, a little bedraggled now, but still beautiful. She put her hand on the bin, and softly called out. There was no reply. A fine rain began to fall. Galadriel ran home, weeping. Or possibly laughing.

He was finally rescued by Jim, the old caretaker. Jim took the thing that had once been the boy under his protection, and when he finally retired, the Dwarf took his place. Jim had been a quiet and secretive man, performing his janitorial tasks with invisible efficiency, but the Dwarf became even more elusive. He was a shade, a ghost, a spirit.

At times you could hear him squirming through the air-conditioning ducts. You'd see him, sometimes, from the corner of your eye, polishing furtively, but when you'd turn to get a proper look, he'd vanish. Sometimes a manic clanging would come from the big metal bins, but when the teachers rushed to the scene, they would find no one there.

But we knew that he was watching everything, listening to everything, a shrunken, fearsome, omniscient god.

And we knew where he lived.

CHAPTER TWENTY-ONE
An Orpheus For the Underworld

IN this story all roads lead to the Interzone. But now I was headed to a place beyond the Interzone. To the dark heart of the dark heart. This early in the day the Interzone was almost deserted: no freaks or zombies or mutants or Lardies or Bacon-heads. No dirty fingers pawed at me. No faces were upturned in supplication, or averted in shame. It was just an alleyway. It almost made me feel as though the other Interzone, the one filled with the helpless and the hopeless was imaginary, the sort of thing my mind used to cook up back when I was ill.

But no. I could still sense the horror, impregnated into the stones and brick and concrete.

I reached the place: a rusting iron grating at the

bottom of the wall. I clutched it and the flakes of rust cut into my hands. Someone was pulling at my blazer. I looked down to see Rat Zermatt. He must have followed me here.

"No, not good. Not good at all. Go there not come back. The Dwarf – he – he…"

I shoved him away.

"I need to know what's going on. The truth is here. The truth is underneath. The truth is – is the Dwarf."

A final wrench and the grate came away. Rat still clutched at me with tiny rodent hands as I crouched and scraped through the opening. Then I dropped down two metres, landing in a puddle of scummy water. I was in a narrow tunnel. The only light down here was cast by dim red security bulbs. It was like being trapped in a stricken submarine.

I put my hand onto the wall: old brick, slimy with mould and weird fungal growths. One way seemed to lead only to a yet deeper gloom. In the other direction I sensed an open space. I moved towards it.

I was in the Underworld: the labyrinth of channels and passageways under the school. It all dated back to Victorian times. Our school was built on the site of an old workhouse – a sort of prison where you got sent for the crime of being poor. There were stories about the terrible things that went on there. Murdered children buried under the foundations. Spectres. Horrors. Monstrous things without a name.

The gas, electric and plumbing for our school all ran through the basement and whenever workmen went down there they'd always emerge looking ashen, and none could ever be induced to return. Sometimes they'd talk of the tiny, fleeting, twisted figure they'd seen, or thought they'd seen, swinging above them on electrical cabling, or disappearing down a side tunnel. I'd been down here once before, back in the days when I had friends. A bunch of us did it for a dare. We laughed and joshed and pushed each other, and nothing happened. But we didn't linger. Now I was alone, and running away wasn't an option.

I reached the big space I'd sensed. It was being used as a storage area for old school junk: mysterious machines with handles and drums from the time before photocopiers and computers; broken desks with blackened, built-in inkwells; outdated gym stuff – quoits and dumbbells. Something about the space made me think it had once been the exercise yard from the old workhouse, crushed now by the building above it into this subterranean existence. I half imagined that I could hear the desolate laughter of long-dead children, playing barefoot in the snow.

And then I heard something else. The sound of

movement. Stealthy and yet swift. Somewhere above me. In the vaults, in the mess of wires and pipes and inscrutable tubing.

Behind.

No, in front.

My hair stood on end. I called out. "Dwarf, I need to talk."

A hiss. Laughter? A curse?

"Come."

The voice, that word, was the single most terrifying thing I'd ever encountered. Ancient, yet childlike. Evil and innocence compacted. I was frightened. Truly frightened. It was the sort of fear that stalks us in our dreams, but now the dream world and the waking one were together, and the morning would not save me.

"Come."

"Come where? Come how?" My voice was cracked and feeble.

"Come."

I found that I was walking through the space, drawn deeper into the nightmare. There was something in the far corner. Some kind of … *structure*. Boxes arranged. What looked like pillars. Almost like a temple or a tomb. No, a shrine. Or a sacrificial altar. There were candles.

"Come."

The voice was so close it could almost have been

inside my head. I wanted to run, to scream, to wake up, but all I could do was to shuffle forward, down and back through time. Back to the tomb, the shrine, the altar. I was close now. The candles had burnt low. There were three walls built from junk and a sort of roof. The fourth side was open. In one corner there was a rolled-up sleeping bag and a filthy pillow.

Standing in the middle was one of the old school desks. I was close now and I could see something on the desktop. Something almost like a bird's nest. A metre away I stopped. The nest was made of golden hair, woven in a circle. In the middle of the circle was a faded black-and-white photograph. It was creased and torn, and I could only just make out the contours of a face that might once have been beautiful. I stretched out my hand to pick it up.

And then again I sensed the movement above me. Too late I tried to run, and a weight hit my head and shoulders. I staggered to my knees. I felt tiny, coarse hands over my eyes. I was blind.

"Naughty naughty. No touching."

The voice was right in my ear. Someone, something was squatting on my shoulders. I hauled myself to my feet, and tried to shake the demon off.

"Dwarf, I mean you no harm. I just want to talk, to ask you—"

Harsh laughter cut me off.

"Mean *me* no harm? *He he ho ho*, that's a good one. Couldn't do *me* harm. But I can harm you, oh yes."

Then I could see again, as the Dwarf's little fists pummelled the top of my head and scrunched at my ears and pulled my hair. I bellowed and reached up to drag him off. But he held on tenaciously. I ran around the room, tossing my head, pushing, jabbing, hitting. Anything to free myself from his grip. Then I felt him lower his mouth to my ear:

"Stay still or I bite it off. I likes an ear. Very chewy."

I felt his teeth clamp around the top of my ear. Felt the sharp pressure. Felt blood begin to trickle. I stopped running and let my arms drop to my sides.

"Good boy," he said, soothingly, as if to a dog.

"I need to ask—"

"Again, asking, asking, asking. Did I ask to be like this? Asking isn't getting. Did I ask for a flesh that grips my twisted skeleton like teeth? Did I ask for these clumsy fat hands like toads? Did I ask for the bell, the great bell that rings for ever in my head? Ask not for whom the bell tolls. It's a-tolling for me and my girl."

Then more hysterical laughter, like the howling of an ape. And all the time he pummelled my head and gouged at my eyes, and squeezed my face with his bony knees.

"Well, Johnny Middleton, you're all alone here now, aren't you? No man is an island, except the Isle of Man, *ho ho ho*. And you. Alone, an island, and just me on the island. A little king. A little emperor. The Napoleon of you."

"One question … please, that's all—"

"And now he's pleasing me with his plea of please."

I was still staggering about under the Dwarf, and my foot kicked something that skittered away across the floor. I looked down. Bones – of what? The dead. The bones are always of the dead. I was losing … losing what? My mind? Consciousness? I had to do something or I would be bones. Nothing but bones.

And then I remembered that Hobnob had given me a name, and names have powerful magic.

I made myself speak.

"Leo. Leo Pardi—"

The creature screamed again. But now it was a different sound: a high, unearthly sound of anguish, the sound of a soul that knows itself damned. I spoke on through the keening.

"I know your name. I know that you are not a demon. I know that you are not the Dwarf, or not merely the Dwarf. I know that you are a human being. I know that you have suffered. I know that you are good."

"Not good. Evil. Made evil. Made ugly."

"No, made human, made free, made noble. And because you are free and because you are noble, you will tell me what I need to know. You must. I gave you back your name."

The Dwarf made another noise. Not a scream this time. It was the sound a lost child makes to comfort itself in the forest, a tuneless hum for ever on the verge of epic sadness.

"The one who brings death."

"Yes."

"The murderer of the innocent."

"Yes."

"Not who you think."

"Then who?"

"The higher power. The smiling god. The benevolent devil. The lost queen. Paracelsus in his alchemical laboratory."

With each word the Dwarf's voice became both more urgent and yet fainter, as if the effort of speaking were draining him of his life force. And suddenly I felt him go limp. He fell from my shoulders and would have crunched to the ground had I not caught him.

I looked for the first time at his face. It was ageless and ancient, young as a spring flower, yet old as Osiris. His eyes were closed. He was mumbling. I put my ear to his lips.

"The shrine." Just a breath. *"Countess."*

I carried him to the shrine that he had built to his love and laid him down on the old school desk. He coiled around the nest of bright hair and he reached for the photograph. His fingers closed around it and drew it to his breast.

"Go," he said.

I turned and began to pick my way across the room. Then I stopped, partly because my eyes had blurred. I turned again and went back to the tiny form of Leo Pardi. I picked him up once more and cradled him in my arms. For the first time he opened his eyes. Even under the dim red lights they glowed with an intense green fire. They were extraordinary. They were truly, truly beautiful. His mouth moved again, but I could make nothing of the whispered breath. Slowly I carried Leo out of the Underworld, and he did not look back.

We emerged into the Interzone. Time had passed. There were people. The addicts and the lost souls parted before us. We moved into the sun, and as we did, the frail body in my arms became ever lighter. I looked up into the blue sky – the first blue sky that I could remember in a long time – and then down again at Leo. But what had been Leo was melting into the air. His eyes closed again for the last time, and I bent and kissed his cheek. My tears were flowing freely now, so that I could hardly see him. And then it seemed that I saw or felt his spirit begin to rise. I looked up and the sun dazzled through the tears, and when I looked down there was nothing in my arms but a pile of stinking rags with a circle of hair and a faded photograph, and soon even these became dust and passed into the air.

CHAPTER TWENTY-TWO
The Collector

I sat on a bench. There aren't any words for what I was feeling. Music, sad music, maybe, but no words.

"Hey, Middleton."

I looked up. It was Hart, as cool and perfect and unreadable as ever.

"Hello," I said, my voice betraying my uncertainty.

"The Principal wants to see you," he said, blandly.

"Now?"

"Yeah, now. In his office."

"How'd you find me?"

"Rat said he saw you down there." Hart nodded towards the Interzone. "Why you holding those rags?"

I looked down at the scraps of filthy cloth in my hands. I couldn't think of anything to say in answer to Hart's question, so I just walked over and dumped them in the big metal bin outside the school kitchens.

As we walked, Hart spoke.

"Dorothy wants to know if you've got anywhere. With the chickens and guinea pigs. She's worried. We're all worried."

I gave him a stare. I tried to give the impression that I knew things. "I've got some leads. Shouldn't be long now."

I was watching his eyes closely. His pupils dilated a little.

"Anything concrete I can give Dorothy? She's getting … tetchy. If they cancel the play … well, it's not going to be pretty. I'm on your side, Middleton, but you need to help me to help you."

"Tell her I'll be in touch soon."

He looked like he was going to say something else, but then swallowed it. "OK," was all that came out. Then he walked on, his movement so smooth he might have been on skates.

I'd never been in the Principal's office before. I hesitated outside, and then knocked, weakly. There was no reply, so I knocked again, too hard this time.

"Enter."

Mr Vole was sitting behind a huge old desk. It

looked like it might have belonged to the master in the old workhouse days. Vole's hands were together, as if in prayer, and he rested his chin on the tips of his fingers. I noticed the brown liver spots on his hands.

Vole stared at me, looking perplexed. His watery eyes searched around the room for any help with guessing who I was, or what I might possibly want. He appeared to have aged since I'd last seen him. He could have been a thousand years old. I took the opportunity to check out the room. The first thing that caught my eye was the large glass vivarium, home to our school tortoise, the Venerable Bede himself. The tank was filled with variegated foliage and dominated by a broken, barkless log. It took me a couple of seconds to locate the tortoise. He was staring out from beneath the log, utterly motionless. I thought, briefly, that he might already have been assassinated – poisoned, perhaps, or pierced with a paralyzing dart. But then he half turned and retreated back into his jungle fastness.

Next to the vivarium there was a gnarled bonsai tree in a terracotta pot. A pair of sharp pruning shears nestled at the base. The tortoise, the tree, the head teacher: three ancient specimens hanging on past their time.

Still Vole said nothing, so I looked at the walls, which were full of certificates and old photos. One photo showed what might have been Vole as a young man, wearing a white lab coat. I recalled that he had once been a chemistry teacher, back in the days when he had something useful to contribute. There was a photo of what could have been the cast of a school play: rows of flower-garlanded boys, dressed in hula skirts. And, taking up almost half of one wall, there was a huge framed picture of hundreds of butterflies, arranged in a tight grid.

"Ah...?"

"It's Middleton, sir. You asked to see me."

The fog cleared a little.

"Yes, to do with...?"

"The animals, sir. The stick insects. And the guinea pigs. And now the chickens."

"Oh, yes, yes, yes, bad business. You were there, this morning, of course you were. Poor creatures. You are the boy accused by Mr Shankley of involvement. No insight into character, Mr Shankley. He seems to believe that rules are all you need. But he doesn't ... which is to say, and I'm sure you'll agree, that I do. I knew that you were never ... that you hadn't ... and so I asked you to... Anyway, did you have any luck? Getting to the ... ah, bottom?"

"I've got a couple of ideas."

"Ideas? Oh, good, yes, excellent. Except that, ah,

well, this all seems a little, how shall I say, *posthumous*. Insofar as most of our beloved school menagerie is now *deceased*."

"There's still the tortoise." I pointed at the glass tank.

"Eh? Oh. Of course. Dear, dear Bede. The last survivor. Still safe in our, as it were, bosom. You know, I'm sure, the story of the retreat from Kabul in 1842? Thirteen thousand soldiers and camp followers set off. All were massacred by the tribesmen, save for one. And even he had half his head sliced off by a scimitar. Somehow the fact that there was a single survivor made the whole, ah, tragedy more, erm, tragic."

His eyes misted over, while he went on his own retreat from Kabul. He even flinched a couple of times, as bullets whizzed past his ears and ricocheted off the rocks. Finally he nodded sadly to himself, and then looked at me as if he'd never seen me before in his life.

"Sir?"

"What?"

"Was there something you actually wanted to ask me, sir? Something you wanted me to do?"

"Do? Yes, of course. Hope."

"You want me to hope?"

"Want you to hope? No, not much use in just hoping. I mean to say, that as long as the Venerable

Bede is alive then hope lives. Hope that the show will go on. That great and noble institution. Part of school history. Part of – part of… Well, anyway, good work, ah, Munton."

"Middleton."

"That's right, that's right. Keep it up. Report back when there is, when you, when, ah, well…"

"Sir."

I stood up and turned to go. As I did I took a closer look at the butterfly picture. It wasn't. A picture, I mean. There was too much texture, an excess of the third dimension. The butterflies were real. Dead and mounted in the frame. Beautiful. And creepy. It looked like another one of the relics from the workhouse days. Perhaps one of the old Masters had been a butterfly collector.

"Lovely, aren't they? My hobby. Since I was a young boy…"

I felt a sudden ripple of … what? Revulsion? No, too strong. It was just a bit creepy. I wasn't even sure what the "it" was – the dead insects in the picture or something in my own head? But I couldn't yet drag myself away from the butterflies. They seemed … significant. And then, as I gazed, the shapes in the picture changed. Butterflies no longer, I saw tiny images of the other dead creatures of the school. And then a face staring out, returning my gaze with dead eyes. It was me, there, pinned to the board.

Vole was suddenly behind me. He put a hand on my shoulder and said something which I did not catch. I took it as a dismissal and, longing for breathable air, I got out of there as fast as I could.

And bumped right into the Shank himself, who was just emerging from his own room. He pierced me with a glare that could have done good work with the Spanish Inquisition.

"Middleton. What are you doing here?"

"Mr Vole asked to see me, sir."

A slight pause. Then "In there!" He opened his door for me.

I didn't have a lot of choice. I went in and sat down.

"Get up."

He hustled behind his desk, where he clearly felt more comfortable.

"Sit down."

I sat.

The Shank considered me. I considered him back. His face changed, slackening slightly, as if he were releasing the contents of a full bladder. I guessed it was the Shank trying to appear pleasant. It obviously took a lot of effort.

It also took a lot of effort for me not to look into

those green eyes and see his lovely daughter.

"Look, *John*," he said, in a way that was almost friendly. "It's no secret that you've been … unwell."

"That was ages ago. I'm fine now."

"I've been trying to contact your parents."

"They're away."

"Away? For how long?"

"Back tomorrow. They're at a funeral."

"Ah, I see. My concern is that your problems have returned. We think that you might need some help."

It was a good trick. The Shank knew that brutality couldn't break me, so he was trying the velvet glove.

"This is because you still think I'm the one responsible for killing the pets?"

"Tell me, John, what would you think in my position? We have a boy with known psychiatric issues—"

"I told you, I'm better now."

"*With known psychiatric issues*, who happens to have been on or near the scene of a number of acts of senseless violence."

"Senseless? You sure?"

"Yes, senseless. Random acts of cruelty." The Shank sighed. "All *I* want to do is to clear this up so the school can get back to normal. All *you* have to do is to tell me the truth. I'm a fair man, and if you confess I'll make sure the whole matter is treated with discretion."

"Discretion?"

"If I can, I'll keep the police out of this. You may not even be expelled. A short period of suspension may be all that's necessary. It will be an opportunity for you to get some help."

"That's kind of you, Mr Shankley. Real kind. But we both know that you've got nothing. That's what this is *really* about. And I've another idea I'd like to run by you. When you have a crime and you can't find an obvious perp, then you have to ask yourself a question. Who stands to gain? I mean why would anyone want to kill the school pets?"

Shankley didn't like to be challenged and the mask, so recently put on, slipped.

"Perverts, freaks … you people don't need a reason beyond your own sick inclinations."

"Sure, it suits you to have everyone believe that these are random acts. But let me answer my own question. The person who stands to gain most from this mess is you."

There was a famous, rarely encountered, final stage to Shankley's fury. The stage where he spoke quietly. He was there now.

"Enough."

"Not nearly enough. You hate the Queens. Losing

the show will break them, and that means you and your bully-boys will have total control."

If you'd given me the option, I'd have said all that in a pleasant, calm voice. I think I may have been a touch more *emphatic* than I'd intended. Anyway, the Shank's face remained immobile, except for the tiniest hint of a tremor in his eyelid.

But I still hadn't finished. Shank was a rotten tooth and I had to shove my probe in and stab at the nerve.

"You talk about freaks, but no one's born a freak. Look at what you've done to your own daughter, how you've messed her up..."

I didn't really know what I was getting at, I just wanted to goad the Shank. It worked. Sorta. His face became ashen and wore an expression of bewilderment and fear. And then he pulled his features back into line.

"I have no daughter," he said, as stern and cold as the statue of a Roman emperor.

"Yeah, sure," I said. "And I spend my evenings talking to myself in coffee shops."

The Shank gave me a stare. He reached over and pressed a red button on his desk. A second later the door opened behind me. "This boy is clearly unwell. I think he needs to lie down. Take him to the sick bay, please."

Then Shankley stood and turned his back on me. He

walked to his window and gazed out over the tussocky green field and onto the redbrick houses beyond. I felt hands on my arms and knew what to expect.

"Playtime," whispered Bosola into my ear.

CHAPTER TWENTY-THREE
SICK BAY BLUES

I was slumped in a chair in the sick bay. My hands were tied behind my back. The old resuscitation dummy was staring me in the face. She'd seen better days. She looked like a one-eyed crack addict, beaten up and left for dead in an alleyway.

But she packed a punch.

Thwack!

It was Funt who was playing puppet-master.

"Wake up, baby," he said in the voice of a trampy resuscitation dummy. "How about a little kissy-kissy?" Then he rammed the dummy's head into my face. Again. And again.

"That'll do, for now," said Bosola, from behind me.

"Yeah, you do what you're told, Funt," I slurred. "I've

had supermarket trolleys with more free will than you."

"You make me laugh, Middleton."

"Nah – to make you laugh now I'd have had to tell you that joke last Sunday."

Funt didn't bother with the dummy this time, just gave me a serious backhanded slap. My face whipped round and a gobbet of blood flew from my mouth and splattered against the padded wall.

"I said that'll do, Funt. He's trying to wind you up. It's all he's got now." Bosola came round to the front. That was where I wanted him. My hands were behind my back, and I had no chance of working them free with him watching.

"Mr Shankley requires some information. You're going to give it to us. Understand?"

I shrugged again. I was working pretty hard at those ropes and shrugging was good cover. I was also thinking. The Dwarf had given me cryptic clues and I had to work them out. The higher power. The smiling god. The benevolent devil. The lost queen. Paracelsus in his laboratory. Were these different people? No, just one, I thought. The lost queen made me think of Emma West. She was a Queen, but she wasn't lost. Paracelsus ... a scientist of some kind. Or maybe an alchemist. Meanings flickered just beyond my reach, like a piano playing in another room.

"He ain't listening," said Funt, and gave me a little shake to get my attention.

"OK. Number one," said Bosola, "why did you kill the stick insects?"

"Because they were there."

Slap. Not too hard.

"You admit you killed them."

"Sure, why not?"

Slap. Harder.

"OK, OK. Look, I like sticks. Sticks are cool. You got a stick, you can use it for anything. And if you break it in half, you haven't got a broken stick, you've got two sticks. It's magic. Just try that with a gun. So, it's not right that stick insects pretend to be what they aren't. They haven't earned it. They had to pay."

"Let's move onto the guinea pigs. Where are they?"

"Inside a fat man."

This time it was a punch. Luckily Bosola was a coward and knew that a punch to my eye socket or chin would hurt him, so it landed on my cheek. It wasn't fun, but it didn't do me any damage.

"The chickens?"

"That was a fox, dummy."

"Someone cut the wire to let the fox in. That was you, wasn't it?"

I shrugged. I was bored. My mind was elsewhere. I

thought for a minute I might be able to imagine away Funt and Bosola, that maybe I was just having a rest here in the quiet of the sick bay, a refuge of calm from the sound and fury of school life.

But some things you can't imagine away.

"He's off again, boss," said Funt. "Look at his eyes. Someone's blown out his pilot light."

"OK, that's it. I'm going to get his attention. The chief said leave no marks, but screw that."

From what felt like a long way away, I watched Bosola reach into his pocket and take out a gleaming brass knuckle-duster. It had a certain brutal beauty, like the obsidian knives the Aztecs used to cut the hearts from their victims. It caught and reflected the harsh light. Like … like a cat's eye in the night.

"I'm going to punch you now, in the face. Not sure exactly where yet. If I go for your mouth, then I'm afraid those pretty teeth of yours are going to be embedded in the back of your skull. If I go for the jaw, then the bone's gonna crumble like dried-up poodle shit."

He pulled back his hand, like Robin Hood drawing his bow.

It was time to do something. I'd been working on my fetters, but my hands still weren't free. I wrenched and twisted, but there was no way out.

I shut my eyes.

CHAPTER TWENTY-FOUR
The Queen Moves

WHICH meant that I missed the good bit.

Some part of my brain might just have registered the sound of the door opening. Dumb, really, of the two clowns not to have locked it. What my brain certainly registered was the sound of a goon being strangled. That and the fact that I wasn't wearing an imprint of Bosola's knuckle-duster on my face.

I opened my eyes. Bosola was going purple. There was a feathery scarf around his neck. The ends of it were in the finely manicured hands of Emma West, aka Dorothy, aka the Queen Mother. Two other Queens had a hold of Funt and were squeezing the juice out him. In slightly different circumstances he might have enjoyed it. Right now he wasn't enjoying it one bit. In fact, there were tears rolling down his cheeks and he was making a sound like a dying buffalo.

One of the Queens doing the squeezing was a giant marshmallow that I knew by instinct must be my old friend Sophie. Sophie was big and pink, with fizz of curly blonde hair that also had bigness and pinkness in it. I was very glad that whatever it was she had been going to do to me back in the drama studio remained undone.

The other Queen was Hart, looking as effortlessly distant as ever.

Before Bosola passed out, Dorothy pushed him away, using the feather boa to spin him like a top. He rotated into a corner and slumped there like an oversized, pooper-scooped bag of dog waste.

"Well, sugar," said Dorothy. "Looks like we arrived in the nick of time."

"Another thirty seconds and I'd have been eating teeth. So, yeah, thanks."

While I was speaking, Sophie and Hart were disentangling me from the chair and helping me up.

"Let's get gone," Dorothy said, looking with distaste at the resuscitation dummy and the two goons. "This place gives me the heebies. Reminds me too much of home."

Leaving Funt and Bosola to nurse their wounds, we

hit the corridor. Luckily the Shank was still safely in his room, waiting, no doubt for his Inquisitors' report. But as we went past, the Principal's door suddenly opened, and Mr Vole appeared, as crumpled and disoriented as ever. He looked successively at the three Queens and me, and seemed to have a new level of mystified bafflement for each one.

"Er … ah … urm…" he managed, before Dorothy swept up to him, air-kissed him with a loud *mwah mwah*, added a quick, "Darling, adore the hair. Love to stay and chat but the last dress-rehearsal beckons" and then swept on, carrying us in her slipstream.

"I don't mean to show a lack of gratitude," I said as we strode along, "but, well, why?"

"Why help you? Isn't it obvious? You were supposed to be tracking down whichever lowlife is putting our show at risk."

"But I thought you suspected me?"

"Perhaps I did. But let's just say you made a certain … *impression* at our last meeting." She cast a sidelong glance at Sophie, who responded with a blush so deep you could sink a battleship in it. She looked down and twisted her hands together and screwed one toe into the floor.

"Sophie's a little on the shy side," Dorothy continued, arching one eyebrow in a way you'd have to say was pretty cool. "But she knows how to show a boy a good time. If you ever wanted some company…"

"I'll take a rain check," I said, a little too quickly, and then felt like a heel. So I gave Sophie a soft look and added, "I'll buy you a coffee when this is all over."

You'd have thought it impossible, but her blush took on an even greater intensity. Like on a U-boat hiding on the bottom from the patrolling destroyer, rivets were starting to pop.

Suddenly a thought struck me. Rat Zermatt, talking about "she" with that edge of terror in his voice… I'd always assumed that the "she" was Zofia, paying me back for hiding those guinea pigs.

"It was you, wasn't it? The warning. About the hit…?"

Dorothy shrugged. "You were batting for us. I didn't like the thought of that cute nose of yours getting all bent out of shape." As she spoke, she reached out and touched my nose. It was my turn to blush.

"And besides," she continued in a grimmer tone, devoid of all flirtation, "anything Paine and the Lardies were mixed up in had to be wrong."

"Ain't that the truth," I added.

So, I'd been wrong about Zofia. If I had a guardian angel, it was blowsy, loud-mouthed drama royalty, not my enigmatic emo. How many other things might I have been wrong about? Since I'd been born, we were probably up into the zillions. I was also thinking that since I'd stopped taking my pills things were getting clearer. I was seeing things that I missed before. Making connections.

"But," I continued, "I don't think the Lardies are at the bottom of this. Paine was on a commission. You got any idea who set it up? If we find that out, then we've got our guy."

She shook her head.

"I had Hart here keep a look out for you. He heard nothing. But then a rumour came through the vine. I don't know how it started… You got any leads?"

I thought again about the Dwarf and what he'd told me. Played it over in my head for the thousandth time.

"Just got a cryptic crossword clue, and I suck at crosswords."

Emma West smiled. "Hart's good at puzzles. Why not run it past him?"

I looked at Hart. He was looking at nothing.

"Well, it's kinda goofy."

"Look around you. It's a goofy world we're in."

"OK."

So I sort of chanted, trying to get a laugh: *"The higher power, the smiling god, the benevolent devil. The lost queen. Paracelsus in his laboratory."*

I was watching Hart as I spoke. As I've said, he wasn't so much a closed book, as a book with nothing but blank pages. But I thought I saw something written there now. Just an indistinct pencil line, there for a second, and then erased. What was it that got him – the queen? The laboratory?

He made a little rippling movement with his shoulders, like an armless man trying to scratch the back of his neck.

"This isn't like a crossword clue," he said, "where you have all you need, and there's only one answer. It's just vague ... ideas, suggestions. But, I don't know, the higher power sounds like the Shank. And Paracelsus, well, he was a doctor and alchemist and that could sort of be Mrs Maurice, who's the nearest thing to a lab junky I know."

He was hiding something. He hadn't mentioned the queen. I looked at Emma West again. Certainly a Queen. Was she mixed up in this in ways I couldn't fathom? Was it some political power play? Was she using me, just like the others? It made no sense.

My thoughts never got anywhere because at that moment we had a pleasantly distracting bit of comic theatre. We were on the stairs by now. Suddenly Hart, who was ahead of us, let out an extraordinary scream-cum-yelp and leapt into the accommodating arms of

Sophie. Sophie was strong enough to carry three Harts, but the shock made her stagger, causing her to miss the step. She began to topple backwards, still holding Hart in her arms like a doll. I braced myself and caught her. Even then we'd probably all have ended up in a broken heap at the bottom of the stairs had Dorothy not added her surprising strength to the battle. Sophie regained her balance, but Hart still wouldn't climb down. He had his head burrowed in Sophie's ample bosom.

"Bug," he whimpered, "bug."

And then we saw it: an admittedly quite impressive cockroach was scuttling back and forth on one of the stairs. Dorothy tutted and kicked it into the stairwell. She looked at me in an exaggeratedly world-weary way. "He's such a cry-baby when it comes to creepy-crawlies."

The cockroach was big enough for me to hear a faint click as it landed a couple of floors down. A faint click that rang an even fainter bell somewhere in the back of my mind.

"Got to go," I said. "Something to check out."

CHAPTER TWENTY-FIVE
Two Clues For Comfort

THE link connected me back to the beginning of this whole mess, and the sound of chopsticks being dumped in the bin. But even as my brain made that connection, another thought hurtled in, and demanded, like a spoilt child, to be attended to first.

I ran out of the building and across the schoolyard. The chicken run stood empty and forlorn, like a memorial to some forgotten atrocity. I was praying that no one had been in there to clean up the mess yet, and for once my prayers were answered. The beak, open in silent accusation, was still there. The blood. The feathers.

I scanned the run. There were small, fluffy feathers everywhere, along with some of the longer, flight feathers from the chickens' wings. Then I saw what I was looking for. I'd first seen it just before the mini-riot kicked off that morning, but didn't take in its significance. It was a feather, but one that had never been attached to a chicken. I lay down on the ground and reached in through the hole cut in the wire. At full stretch my fingers found the feather. I slipped it into my wallet.

A few seconds later I heard the bell sound for the end of the day. I hadn't realized the time. *Ask not for whom the bell tolls,* said the Dwarf. Today seemed to have both just begun and yet to have lasted a lifetime. I went to wait outside the school gates.

It wasn't long before I saw her. She was with one friend, a girl called Jiao. Jiao was as plain as Ling Mei was beautiful, and she'd always thought I was a scumbag. Still, it could have been a lot worse. I really didn't feel like fighting all of Chinatown right now.

Ling Mei gasped when I stepped out from the shadows.

"I just need a second."

Jiao made a kind of screeching noise, and then began to curse me in Cantonese. I put my arms up in a soothing gesture, but it didn't stop her from aiming a vicious kick at my shins. Then she ran off back towards the school. I reckoned I had two minutes before she came back with reinforcements.

"Please, Ling Mei – the day you lost your chopsticks, you said anyone could have stolen them. But my guess is, it was someone sitting behind you. It's the easiest way. It's what I'd do if I wanted to take something from your bag. So who was sitting in the row behind you that morning in registration?"

Ling Mei shook her head sadly. But I could tell she was trying to remember.

"Why don't you just leave this, John? In fact, why don't you just leave full stop? You need to start fresh somewhere. Somewhere without a history. Some place where everyone doesn't hate you. Where they don't know about your past, about the time you were ill."

I won't pretend those blows didn't hurt. They were low, and they detonated like mortar bombs in my guts. But I could take a blow, even a low one.

"*Who*, Ling Mei, *who*?"

A sigh. And then, "Right behind me there's Steve Sutcliffe. Behind to the left, it's Paul Ehrlich. Behind to the right, Julia Walsh. Happy?"

No, I wasn't. I was expecting another name. It showed on my face.

"Did they have to be behind?" Ling Mei asked, showing a flicker of interest.

"Yes … well … I don't know. Which side was your bag on?"

"You forgot already. Is there anything you remember about me?" For the first time in a long time, the ghost of a smile.

"You're left-handed. So it would be on the left side. Who sits next to you there?"

"Nicholas."

"Nicholas? I don't know a—"

"Hart. Nicholas Hart."

Something made me look back towards the school. They were coming. Jimmy was leading the pack. Ling Mei saw them too.

"Run," she said.

I had no control over what came next. If I *could* have controlled it then it wouldn't have happened, because I knew it was dangerous for her.

I leant over and kissed her on the mouth. Her lips parted and she kissed me back. I could have stayed like that for the rest of my life, and I had the feeling that she felt the same way. Which is why I had to stop.

I whispered into her ear. "Push me away and slap me. Make it look like I forced you."

"No."

Her tears were on my cheek.

"Now, or I'll wait here until they kill me."

A sob clawed its way out of some deep cavern within her.

"Ling Mei, please…"

And then she slapped me, and fell to the ground. I wanted more than anything on Earth to stoop to help her, to hold her, to be with her. But to help her would be to damn her, and so, with the jeers and threats of Jimmy and his gang ringing in my ears, I fled like a coward into the dusk.

CHAPTER TWENTY-SIX
Of Love and Demons

SO, I had the killer. That alien feather in the chicken coop – it was ostrich, and it could only have come from a Drama Queen's feather boa. I'd placed Hart right at the scene of the very first crime – the theft of Ling Mei's chopsticks. It was him. It had to be him.

I reached home and wished my parents were back. I never thought I'd say this, but I missed them. Hey, I even missed my sister. And suddenly their absence seemed weird, sinister. I was suddenly convinced that it was linked to the killings. It was too big a coincidence. I began to construct a massive conspiracy theory in my head, involving the death of my aunt, my parents being lured away, a kidnapping.

And then I laughed at myself. Laughed so hard I

felt light-headed and had to sit down.

I went and brushed my teeth, which sometimes helps to settle my nerves. It didn't work this time. There was something wrong with the light in the bathroom. It picked up some weird colour in my eyes. A sickly sort of hue. It wasn't healthy. It was barely human.

I'd had nothing to eat all day, but I wasn't hungry. Out of habit, I went to the kitchen and opened a can of peaches. I stared at the virulent orange slices. They reminded me of something scooped out of a body during an autopsy. I poured them into the sink, mashing them down the plughole with a wooden spoon. Then I was sorry that I'd wasted the peaches. I should just have put them in a bowl and eaten them later, when I wasn't thinking of death and evisceration and the absence of love.

I couldn't understand why I felt so down. I should have been eight miles high. Hadn't I cracked the case?

Maybe it was because I couldn't work out the motive. I didn't figure Hart for a sicko who just took pleasure in killing – he didn't look like he took pleasure in *anything*. The best I could come up with was that he was working with the Shank to bring down the Queens or, more specifically, Emma West. Maybe he thought that the Shank would put him in her stilettos, acting as his puppet. It made a kind of sense, but not enough to give me the satisfaction of hearing the case click shut.

But I couldn't resist a little smile at the thought of what Dorothy would do when she found out about the plot. The chances were that Hart would be singing like a Munchkin for the rest of his days.

My next step was to get the feather, and the story it told, to the Principal tomorrow morning. He was weak and he was old, but nobody denied that Mr Vole was a decent man. He would do the right thing, I was sure. He would rouse himself from his years of torpor and slap down the Shank.

Or was I just kidding myself? Did he have the nerve, the guts, the moral muscle? Well, tomorrow we'd find out. Either way, I'd done all that I could. My conscience was clean. My work was done.

But there was a grain of sand in the Vaseline. Zofia. I realized that I hadn't seen her all day. I needed to talk to her. I wanted to explain … *about things*. What did I need to explain…? *The important things.* But now I couldn't remember them… My head wasn't working properly. But if I talked to her, it would be better, that much I knew.

I'd call her. We could meet again, like last night. I wouldn't say anything dumb this time. I could tell that she liked me. We did that clicking thing. We would be together. She'd understand and help me. We could save each other.

First I had to call her. But how? I'd never taken down her number. Numbers started to whirr in my head like a slot machine. I knew that when they stopped I'd have hers. I tried to stop the spinning numerals, but I couldn't even slow them.

I slapped my head to *make* the numbers stop. I was missing something. Yes, that was it: I hadn't called her, but she'd called me. Our phone had a little LCD screen that showed the last ten calls received.

I scrolled through the list. I was looking for a number I didn't recognize. Mum's mobile. Dad's mobile. Those two numbers repeated over and over again. And then I saw what I was looking for. I probably should have got my thoughts together before I hit redial, but my finger did the thinking.

Three rings.

"Hello," said a voice I didn't recognize. Then some more words that I didn't catch. The voice was Eastern European and unfriendly.

"Pardon?" I said, bewildered.

"Manston Dry Cleaners. Can I help you?"

Dry cleaners...? Maybe she worked there.

"Zofia. Is Zofia there?"

"Zofia? No, no Zofia work here."

I put the phone down. Were they lying? Was this part of it, part of the plot? The boring, obvious answer was that my mum had left some dry cleaning there, and they had just called to tell her that it was ready. But if we always settled for the obvious answer, we'd still think the sun went around the Earth and that it was OK to make margarine out of whales.

But I'd lost my link, and I felt Zofia fading, slipping away. I reached for her through time and space, like the astronomers looking for messages from alien civilizations.

And I heard something, and I knew where she was. I went up on the roof.

CHAPTER TWENTY-SEVEN
The White, the Red, the Blue

"YOU?" I said.

"Who else were you expecting?"

The cat came over and rubbed herself against my ankle. I noticed that my feet were bare and dirty, as if I'd been walking around all day without my shoes on.

"Oh … no one, I guess."

"The girl?"

"The girl? No… Maybe."

"You know, don't you?" said the cat, climbing up onto my knees. That made me feel calmer. Maybe that was the point of cats, you know, why we invented them.

"Me," I said. "I don't know jack shit. So tell me, what should I know?"

The cat thought for a moment.

"That we're all connected."

"Just my luck – my cat's a hippy. Bet you do yoga and drink fruit tea."

"There," she said, pointing her nose at the city. "What do you see?"

"Lights," I said, looking at the pools and points of orange and yellow spilling from houses and cars and streetlamps.

"Not *lights*," said the cat. "*Light*. You think they are each separate, but it's an illusion. Imagine one great light, and a screen of black silk is set before it, and in the screen there are tiny holes. It looks to you as if they are all individual, and isolated, one from the other. But if you could take away the screen, you'd see that there was only one light."

"Nice," I said. "But I don't get what you're trying to say."

"That what you think are separate things are really the same thing. The girl. The Dwarf. The…"

There was a pause into which I inserted the word: "Cat…?"

The cat looked at me, her lovely green eyes full of meaning and yet unreadable.

"It's over with the girl, isn't it," I said. I don't know how I knew it, but I knew it.

"It was over before it started," said the cat. "But you've still got me."

The cat dug her claws into my thighs and coiled further into me.

"Your lap feels bony," she purred. "You can't live on canned peaches, you know."

"Don't give me the peach preach. I get enough of that from … the others."

"It's only because they care about you."

"If they cared they'd be here."

"But they are here … the voices."

"That's the TV."

"Really?"

"And if they cared they wouldn't try to control my thoughts."

"How could they do that?"

"The white pills. The red pills. The blue pills. Sit still, don't fidget."

"I'm cold. You give off no warmth."

"Hmm. You know that movie, the one where the guy dies but doesn't realize it, and just goes on same as before?"

"No."

"Oh, well."

"What will you do?"

"Tomorrow? Finish it, I guess. Tell Mr Vole. Tell

them all. Bring the whole stinking, corrupt edifice crashing down."

"Did you ever worry that the thing behind the edifice might be worse than the edifice?"

"Like a beauty spot over a smallpox pustule?"

"Yes, just like that."

"That's someone else's problem. I'm only trying to get at the truth. What was it you said, about taking away the screen and showing the light behind?"

"You're twisting my words. I was talking about the connectedness, but you're talking about the truth, as if it were a simple, single thing, hiding underneath, or inside the world, like a pearl in an oyster. But that isn't how truth works. All we have are signs. And each sign just points to another sign. There is no pearl, no secret inner truth, no reality behind the edifice. Just the endless play of signs."

"Sounds deep."

"That's cats for you. Scratch me."

"Where? There?"

"Yes, just there."

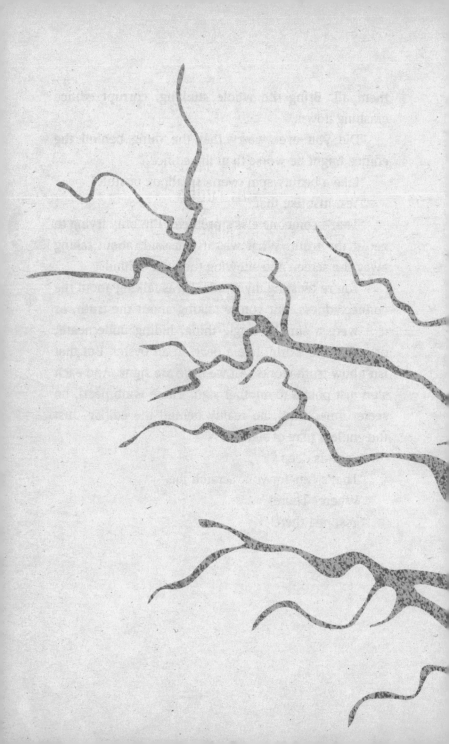

DAY FOUR
Friday

CHAPTER TWENTY-EIGHT
The Counsellor

I woke up on Friday morning knowing two things. The first was that this was the Big Day. The second was that I was late. I pulled my uniform on and ran through the streets, splashing through puddles of black water.

The deserted schoolyard felt vaguely post-apocalyptic. My plan was to go to see the Principal straight after morning registration, so that he could then make his move before the Friday Assembly at twelve. I couldn't say that I had complete confidence in Vole's ability to take the Shank down, but at least I'd have done my part and shucked off the responsibility onto somebody else's shoulders. There was a sort of comfort in that.

I opened my form room door and synchronicity

chimed: Mr Vass was reading out my name from the register. Every kid swivelled towards me. You'd have thought I'd come in wearing a pirate's costume, complete with squawking parrot.

"Ah, John," said Vass. "Good timing. Take a seat."

Not a word about being late. I knew right away that the class had been talking about me. Before he went on with the register, Vass scribbled something on a piece of paper and gave it to a runty kid on the front row. Spellman was his name. Spellman scuttled out of the room. I sat down. There were over-the-shoulder glances, part nervous, part excited. Wilson gave me a full leer, wet and foul. He knew something. They all knew something.

Mr Vass had reached the end of the register when there was a quiet knock at the door. Spellman ducked in and ran back to his desk at the front, leaving the School Counsellor, Ms Cassandra, in the doorway.

Ms Cassandra was one of those ladies who had gone grey early, but had then stayed put, looking ageless. There was a sparsely haired mole, small but unignorable, in the disputed border territory between chin and jaw.

The Counsellor was the person you went to see if you were having "problems", if you were addicted, aphasic or anxious; boring, bulimic, or bullied; cuckolded, cankered or crucified (I could go on…).

Of course the only reason anyone *actually* went to see Ms Cassandra was if it meant they could use the good old excuse of being crazy to get out of games or avoid some punishment. Maybe a few kids feigned insanity to get attention. But you'd have to be mad to do that. Whatever your problem, anorexia or athlete's foot, the gig was the same: Ms Cassandra would ask you how things were at home and try to get you to talk about your feelings. Then she'd hand you a leaflet on safe sex and you'd be on your way.

We'd had a couple of meetings back when my troubles started. It was pretty obvious that whatever I had was out of her league, and I'd sensed ever since that she resented me because of it.

Ms Cassandra (definitely a Ms, by the way – the two states of marriage and singleness seemed equally inconceivable) entered on her sensible heels and engaged in a brief, murmurous interchange with Mr Vass. They both trained their eyeballs on me, and I knew that my plans for the day were about to be rendered obsolete.

"John?" Mr Vass looked a little sorry, as if he'd been hoping for a ham sandwich and it had turned out to be cheese, without even the consolation of pickle.

"Sir?"

"Could you" – he paused, searching for the right verb – "*go* with Ms Cassandra."

His choice seemed not to please him. It amused the class, however, and a long strangulated *WooooOOOOoooooooo!* resulted.

I gathered my gear and followed her out of there.

"What's this all about?" I asked when we were in the corridor.

Ms Cassandra smiled at me. It was a warm, open, understanding smile, and I felt an almost overpowering urge to unfurl the fire hose attached to the wall and give her a blast of high-pressure icy water right in the face.

"It's nothing to worry about. We've heard about some of your recent *issues* and thought that perhaps we'd, well, let things slip. And so I – we – thought it would be good to have a talk."

I suppose I should have sniffed a rat, and I sort of did. But I felt a kind of inertia – you know, that feeling of powerlessness that comes over you, and makes you almost *want* to put yourself in the hands of the authorities.

By now we were at the Counsellor's office. She opened the door. The room was the fanciest in the whole school. There were comfy chairs and a nice carpet and hi-tech blinds over the windows, and the place had that pleasant new-car smell of fresh plastic.

There was even a decent computer – a flatscreen iMac as big as a shop window.

"Please sit down, John," said Ms Cassandra in her soothing voice. "I just need to pop out for a few moments."

She left the room and I flopped into one of the soft chairs. It really was extraordinarily comfy. As I sank into it I couldn't help but let out one of those long sighs that people make when they sit down after some hard task. It was bright in the room, and I closed my eyes to shut out the glare. It was good to sit and let my mind drift.

I was half asleep when the door clicked open. Had I heard the sound of a key turning? Had the Counsellor locked me in? Why would she do that?

She gave me the smile again. She had lovely teeth, clean and white and even.

"Sorry about that, John. I had to make a couple of calls." She sat next to me on a hard chair, pulling her skirt down over her knees. "Now, would you mind if I asked you a few questions?"

"Fire away."

"Have you ever had any pets? Of your own, I mean, not the school animals."

"I don't really see the point of this. But, yeah, we used to have a dog."

"Used?"

"It died."

"How did it die?"

"All dogs die, in the end."

"You mean it died of old age?"

"Something like that, yeah. Cancer maybe. I was little."

Ms Cassandra wrote something down on a pad.

"Any other pets?"

"Not really. Well, sorta. There's a cat that lives on my roof."

"Your roof?"

"Yeah. I feed her, but I don't know if I could call her a pet. You know how it is with cats. You don't own them. They stick around for a while, then they move on. But sometimes it's nice to have someone to talk to."

Ms Cassandra arched her eyebrows. She wrote something down on her pad.

"You talk to your cat?"

"She beats most people as a conversationalist."

There was a slight pause, and then Ms Cassandra tittered, taking it as a joke.

She asked a few more questions, nothing too deep, and I made a couple of wisecracks and she laughed some more. But then I felt like I'd had enough. I had stuff to do. I struggled up out of the comfy chair.

"I have to go," I said. "I've got to—" I stopped myself from saying *get to the Principal.* I didn't want to give my plans away.

For the first time the Counsellor looked uncomfortable.

"We … we think it would be better if you stayed here for a while, John," she replied, not looking at me.

"Who's the 'we'?"

"People who care about you."

Click: I got it. This was all part of the plan to keep me away from Vole.

"Yeah, sure," I said, coolly. "Real caring guy, the Shank."

Ms Cassandra's eyes widened a little. And her fingers moved involuntarily towards the mole on her chin. She took a breath.

"I want you to watch something with me."

"What is it?"

"It's something that I think you need to see."

"Will it take long?"

"Not long."

Ms Cassandra put her hand on my arm and led me over to the iMac in the corner. I won't deny it, I was intrigued. And I reckoned I still had some time. I sat down and the Counsellor leant over to the mouse, giving me a noseful of perfume. In a couple of clicks she had a video running on the screen.

At first it was hard to make out what the hell was supposed to be going on. It was all shadows and murk, like something out of a low-budget horror film. And, just as with a nightmare, the most frightening part was that vague sense of familiarity. I knew this place: the clutter of boxes and unidentifiable objects. A digital clock glimmered in the corner of the computer screen, showing the time that the video was recorded, but I didn't bother to check it. I was too busy peering through the static, trying to work out what I was looking at.

A shape lurched into view, staggering and crashing among the boxes. Whoever it was appeared to be performing a drunken dance. He cavorted to a soundtrack in his head made up of industrial cacophony mashed with death metal. He reached above his head with his hands, grabbing at something, scratching at it, fighting it. But there was nothing there to fight against.

"You know who that is, don't you, John?"

I felt dizzy and nauseous. It was like coming round after a tooth extraction.

"It's... I don't know."

"Do you know *where* it is?"

"It looks like the basement. Under the Interzone."

"Interzone? Interesting... I've never heard of that.

But it is the basement, yes. The storage area. There's a CCTV camera down there. We're looking at the film from the camera. But who is the boy, John? The boy in the film?"

"It's fake," I said.

"How can it be fake? Look at the time and the date, John. Yesterday morning. We know you went down there. People saw you. What are you doing, John? Why are you moving like that?"

"There was someone … someone on my head."

"Who?"

"The Dwarf."

"Dwarf…? John, I—"

"Is this the original?"

"I don't know…"

"It can't be. The surveillance cameras use tape. Someone had to digitize the video so they could put it on the Mac. Once it's been digitized, it's easy to manipulate. Anyone can do it. They've wiped the Dwarf off the movie. You can even see where he was – check out the area above my head, it looks weird. And look at the shadows."

"John, I can't see anything there."

Then I happened to look at the clock on the wall. It was 11.45. How the hell had three hours passed by? The Shank was due to speak to the assembly at 12. I had to get to the Principal to tell him what I'd found out. I stood up, ready to go.

"Just sit down and take it easy," said Ms Cassandra, the tension making her voice harsh.

"I've got a job to do," I said. "There's a boil here that has to be lanced. And I've got the scalpel."

As I spoke I put my hand in my pocket. I don't know why – I just did. But the thing is that Ms Cassandra, who was obviously on the brittle edge of an emotional crevasse, thought I was talking about an *actual* scalpel. A scalpel I was about to use for a bout of impromptu plastic surgery. She shrank back into the corner of the room, screeching out, "Don't cut me! Don't cut me!"

I wanted to explain that, of course, I wouldn't cut her, that there was no scalpel outside the realms of metaphor, and that even if there was I'd never hurt anyone with it, because hurting wasn't my thing. But all that took second place to bringing the truth to Mr Vole. And so I gave Ms Cassandra exactly the kind of sinister look that a scalpel-wielding serial killer might well unfurl the second before getting down to work on the old slice and dice.

She, naturally, moved further away, and I was out through the door before she had the chance to realize that I was bluffing.

CHAPTER TWENTY-NINE
SAFE

I reached Vole's room, panting, thirty seconds later. I'd jinked up and down corridors, making sure that the Counsellor wouldn't figure out where I was going. I knew they'd find me soon enough, but I didn't need long. I slapped at the door, and entered the Principal's office the way a fat kid belly flops into the pool.

Vole was sitting at his desk, gazing at the Venerable Bede, placed before him on his desktop blotter. The tortoise gazed right back. It was like one of those staring competitions: the first one to blink's a sissy.

It was Vole who blinked first. He broke off whatever act of telepathy or mind control he'd been attempting and turned to me. He seemed entirely unsurprised by my sudden appearance.

"Ah, Middlebrow, excellent. I was just about to, er, send for you. Very important job I have for you here. Very important in–ah–deed."

"Sir, I have to tell you—"

"Quite, quite, quite. Of course you do. And all in good, ah, time. But, for now, I need you to stay here as a – a – a *Guardian*. You know, of course, the role of the Guardians in Plato's *Republic*? Yes, of course you do. Philosophers who lead by example. And beyond that, lead by, well, frankly any old way they like. Lying, killing, whatever. Because they have right on their side. The greater good. Yes. Made of gold, unlike the base metal of the mob. Or even the iron – or is it bronze? – of the warriors. Yes, anyway, there you are…"

"Sir, what I have to tell you concerns Mr Shankley and the deaths. I know who—"

"Which is precisely why I need you to stay here. You've done *fine* work, there, Midwitch. Fine, fine work. And now there is the final, ah, the last leg of the, ah, journey. Insofar as waiting here and not moving can be seen as engaging upon a journey, which I believe it can, if you don't take a literal approach to things. Or rather, *words*."

I should have forced my information on him, but there was something curiously reassuring about the old man. Or perhaps it was just something soporific.

Either way, the idea that he had everything in hand had a definite appeal. It meant that the burden was no longer mine to bear alone. Yes, it would all be OK. Mr Vole would see to it. I imagined sinking again into the soft chair in the Counsellor's office.

But, no, that wasn't right. I felt like a prince in a fairy tale, battling an enchantment. I shook my head.

"Sir, it's Hart, he's the one who… I've got proof—"

"I know, my boy, I know. And now you can leave it to me. The important thing is that you stay here and guard our great totem, the symbol of all that the school has come to, ah, symbolize. And stand for. My old friend, the companion of my youth. And age. And we can't take any risks. I'm going to put Bede where no one can reach him."

Then Vole picked up the tortoise and carried him towards the butterflies mounted on the wall. He flicked a concealed latch on one side of the frame and pulled it back. Behind it was a safe. He took a key from his pocket and opened the door. He then placed the Venerable Bede on top of a pile of papers inside the dark womb. Or should that be tomb? Vole's back was towards me and I didn't quite catch what happened next, but I think Vole may have bent and kissed the tortoise's scaly head. Or perhaps he was simply mumbling some words of encouragement or solace to the reptile. Then he shut the door, swung back the butterflies, and turned to me, smiling.

At that moment there came a firm tapping at the door. We both jumped. Miss Bickersniff, the school secretary, half entered.

"Principal, the assembly..." She was obviously used to his forgetful ways.

"Right with you, Miss Bickersniff," Vole replied cheerfully. He turned to me again. "Give me your hand, my boy."

I held out my hand. Vole pressed the safe key into my palm and closed my fingers around it.

"A great responsibility. Keep this safe. Keep *him* safe. Keep *us all* safe. I go now to battle against the forces of, ah, evil. We both know who it is that must be stopped. Cabined, cribbed, confined, to quote the, ah, immortal, er, Bard. Of Avon, that is. Where else, indeed? If anyone at all tries to gain entry, then resist them with all your might and main. I have your word?"

I nodded.

"Principal Vole..." nagged Miss Bickersniff, still waiting.

"Yes, yes, yes. Wonderful. Goodbye, and good luck."

Then the old guy shook my hand, picked up a battered old briefcase, bulging no doubt with unread documents and papers and half-eaten pork pies, and left.

CHAPTER THIRTY
THE FINAL CLUE

THE silence after the thunk of the closing door was like the infinite stillness between the flash of a nuclear detonation and the arrival of the soundwave. There was nothing in the universe apart from that silence. And because even time was beyond the reach of the silence, it felt as if it would last for ever; that sound had been taken out of the world just as you could take an appendix or a spleen or a heart out of a patient.

And then the unnatural silence faded into the familiar quiet of ticking clocks and distant engines and muted birdcalls, and I was left feeling slightly silly. I hadn't given Vole my evidence. But then he didn't seem to need it. Had greater minds than my own grappled with the case and found the solution? Was I truly superfluous?

I didn't know what to do with myself. I sat in one of the guest chairs. Then I sat in Mr Vole's chair. I gazed out of the window. Rows of houses. Four squat tower blocks of grim council flats. You could buy whatever you wanted in there, as long as what you wanted was sex or drugs. A sky made up of a thousand shades of dark grey. Somewhere in the world there was probably a connoisseur of greys, a collector of grey paintings, of grey statues, grey thoughts; he'd have loved it here.

I looked at the things on Mr Vole's desk. You'd have expected it to be cluttered and muddled and chaotic like the guy's brain. However it was almost psychotically neat. There was the large blotter in the middle of the desk, a penholder to one side, a squared-off stack of papers, a laptop. No stains, no biscuit crumbs, none of the tat and meaningless accretions that most desks build up over time. None of the stuff that says, *Hey, this is what I am.*

I opened the desk drawers. Half hoped I'd find something exciting in there: Vole's collection of Edwardian erotica, perhaps, or an automatic pistol, complete with silencer. But it was just more office stuff: staples, elastic bands, a bundle of what looked like receipts. For want of anything better to do, I thumbed through them. About halfway down there was one from a place called Pete's Pets. It said:

1 t. cadaver. £4.

I had no idea what it meant. Then I snorted at the thought that I was so bored I was reading receipts.

I tried to imagine what was going on down in the hall. But my mind was full of … other things. It was snowing static in there like TV reception at the North Pole. And when the static cleared, I saw things I didn't want to see.

I thought about splitting, but Vole had been so adamant that I should stay. He must be expecting some sort of raid on his office, an attempt on the life of the tortoise. Assassins. Who? Hart? Yes, but not just him this time. Bosola and Funt would be there. Could I fight them all off? Hell, yeah.

I got up and wandered around again. I looked at the photo of Vole as a young man in his lab coat. It was the same face, but subtly different. Not just the fact that he was thirty years younger. He looked intelligent, ambitious. I suppose you need a certain ambition to become a Principal, even in a crap heap of a school like ours.

I moved on and found myself in front of the butterflies. You couldn't deny their beauty. Each pinned specimen had a Latin name underneath, often bigger than the butterfly itself. *Ochlodes sylvanus; Gonepteryx rhamni; Lycaena phlaeas eleus.*

Vole must have really loved these things to collect and preserve them like this.

And then I began to think about how odd it was to love something and yet want to kill it. Did he do the deed himself, I wondered, or would he … well, I didn't know what the alternative was. Of course he killed them himself.

And I remembered something.

Mrs Maurice… The correct way to kill insects.

Ethyl acetate.

And I heard the Dwarf's voice. *Paracelsus in his laboratory.* Paracelsus the chemist.

I closed my eyes and leant forwards till my forehead touched the glass covering the dead insects.

Stupid.

Stupid.

Stupid.

Vole. It was Vole.

The Principal had played me like a ukulele. Like a child, I'd assumed that the bad guy had to be, well, the bad guy. I should have realized that it pays for the bad guy to look like a good guy. And if he can't look like a good guy then he can at least look like a fool.

My mouth as dry as a lizard's armpit, I fished

the key from my pocket, threw back the butterflies, plunged the key in the lock and turned. I already knew what I was going to find. The safe would contain a butchered tortoise. He'd used those sharp bonsai-tree clippers to kill it while his back blocked my view. And I was going to be discovered here, holding the tortoise. The dead tortoise. There was no way out. If I ran for it, I'd still get the blame. How could I have been such a dumb-ass?

I opened the safe door, bracing myself for something horrific.

And found … nothing. Apart from the papers, the safe was empty. So was my head. What the hell was happening? Vole must have slipped the tortoise into his pocket while his back was covering the safe. Why? I tried to think it through. It was like a join-the-dots puzzle with all the numbers rubbed out.

Vole's plan was so complicated, so intricate, that I just couldn't fit the pieces together. Not with my mind throbbing and pulsing like a monster in a cheap sci-fi movie. I knew that I couldn't be the main target of Vole's scheming – I just wasn't important enough. This was all aimed somehow at the Shank and the Queens. Nothing else was clear.

But one thing I did know. The empty safe meant that something nasty was planned for the Venerable Bede.

Something nasty and, I guessed, public. On stage – a last great piece of theatre. Well, I had to prevent it. I went to the door.

And stopped.

A thought was nagging at the outer rim of my consciousness. Its shape was still vague, but I could feel it, like a face at a fogged-up window. I forced my brain to work. There was something … something I'd seen. Something that might help.

I returned to Vole's desk, opened the drawer and grabbed the stack of receipts. I found what I was looking for and picked up the phone. As I dialled I happened to glance out of the window. A flash of white and orange caught my eye. A police car was pulling into the drive. Was this part of Vole's plan? And now another vehicle. A white van. No, not a van, an ambulance. For me.

And then a voice in my ear.

"Hello, Pete's Pets. Pete speaking."

CHAPTER THIRTY-ONE
THE CAST ASSEMBLES

THE hall was one of the few impressive things about our school. We'd got lottery funding for it, partly on the back of the growing fame of the theatricals put on by the Drama Queens. There was a wide stage and, in front of it, a seriously big space that could be filled with chairs or cleared for action. At the back of the hall there was a raised level with a sound-and-lighting console, along with floodlights powerful enough to bounce off the moon.

As I approached I felt the hum and buzz from the crowd. Even hushed, there's a noise that comes off a packed mass of kids: the scrunch and rustle of polyester blazers, the coughs and snorts of loosened mucus, the scrape and squeak of shifting chairs.

I crashed through the double doors at the back of the hall and fell smack into the arms of Bosola and Funt. As bouncers, they weren't bad, and they got me in a decent lock. Funt took the opportunity to go for one of his spit-and-punch combos. I ducked the spit, but his fist landed in my guts like a Japanese bullet train. I folded like a deck chair.

But not before I'd taken a snapshot of the whole scene. A thousand kids, near enough, squirming on red plastic chairs. The Shank, centre stage, his skull-like head shining in the spotlight. Vole and a couple of other teachers were seated at one side. The Shank was talking, his voice cold and fierce, like a frozen snarl. "… these appalling events…"

Bosola and Funt still had a hold of me and I saw other prefects coming to their aid. There was no way through here. I twisted out of Funt's grip and repaid a major debt by planting a solid right on Bosola's jaw. It was the neatest, cleanest punch I'd ever thrown. Then I punched him again, a sloppier left. As he fell, I got in a third, a pile-driver down onto his temple. Funt had been admiring my work, but now he grabbed me around my neck, and so I gave him an elbow in the face. Nobody likes an elbow in the face. In a better world elbows and faces would never meet like that. They'd go for a coffee together, maybe, or take in a movie. But this is a bad world, and Funt's nose sprayed blood like champagne after a Grand Prix.

I was thinking fast, my mind, for once, clear. There was a corridor running around the outside of the hall, leading to the stage door. I backed out and ran again, not even checking to see if they were behind me. In fourteen seconds I was at the stage door. I took the set of stairs three at a time, burst through another door, and saw the curtain dividing the backstage from the limelight.

There were other people back here, dull shapes moving in backstage obscurity, but I didn't pay them any attention. I was concentrating on what was out there, centre stage, and what I had to do.

Through a chink in the curtain, I could see the Shank's back, cast in deep shadow by the high spotlight. I could hear him still riffing on the "appalling events". I guessed he was building up to the climax, when he would announce the cancellation of the show and the suppression of the Drama Queens – all because of me. I still couldn't work out Vole's plan in all this.

Just then I saw a second spotlight piercing the gloom, like a clever thought in a dull mind. It was focused away to the empty stage right. I went to the crack in the curtains and looked. The Shank hadn't noticed the new spot, but every eye in the crowd was drawn to the hard, cold circle of light and the horror it contained.

A moan came from the crowd, the way a smell comes from a tramp, unwilled and unwelcome. The Shank, still unaware of what was going on, looked up, trying to find the source of the sound. The moan rose until it became a wail. The wail split into screams.

For a few seconds, the grim-faced Shank still failed to understand what was happening. He was dazzled by his own spotlight, so couldn't see where the hysterical kids were pointing. He checked his fly. He looked to the other teachers on the edge of the stage, but their view of the horror was blocked by the Shank himself. Finally, he turned towards the place where the spotlight fell. I could see his face in profile. The Shank's mouth hung open, as though his brain couldn't quite process the visual information being sent its way.

What he was looking at was a tortoise. But where the wise old head should have been there was nothing but a bloody stump. The severed head had been placed next to the body, where it gazed upon its own demise with a look of stoical acceptance.

That was when I decided to make my move. I swam through the slit in the curtains, meaning to grab the Shank's attention while he was still stunned by the apparition. But he saw me coming. Suddenly he had something useful to do, and he came to life.

"You!" he bellowed. The sound, amplified around the hall, boomed like a starting pistol. "You! You!" he continued, pointing at the dead tortoise. "You did this!"

There are times when terror or excitement can heighten your senses, and now it seemed as though I was seeing the world with supernatural clarity. Looking down I saw that all the players in the tragedy were here. Ling Mei, demure and perfect, sympathy and horror playing over her face; Emma West, in her full Dorothy get-up; Zofia, tall and pale and green-eyed, who looked at me like a ninja assassin, and then smiled, showing her sharp, thin teeth. Mrs Maurice gave me a full-body pout, simultaneously managing to lower her top and raise her skirt by use of will power alone. The Lardy King was there, fat as an opera singer, his lips still greasy with his last meal. Each seemed more real and vivid than the other kids and teachers around them, as if they were made of a different stuff. Not dull, mute matter, but lines of pure thought. Energy given form and substance.

And then there, smiling benignly, was the Principal, Mr Vole.

I walked forwards, but was blinded by the light in my eyes and stumbled. I found that I was at the front of the stage. I had a speech prepared, but before I had uttered a syllable, the doors at the back were thrust open. Two police officers entered, followed by the paramedics from the ambulance.

The headmaster spoke out in a commanding, un-Volelike voice:

"Officers, this is the boy you want. Take him away – but be careful, he may be dangerous."

CHAPTER THIRTY-TWO
THE BRIEFCASE

"GO on, go on," urged the cat. "Don't stop now. Is that when you ran for it? How did you escape?"

I was sitting on my roof. Not sure I could totally tell you how I got there. The cat was in my arms.

It was dark and the lights of the town glowed before me. It would be nice to say that they mirrored the stars, but there were no stars. There are never any stars.

"What? Sorry, I drifted off for a second. Oh, yes. I mean, no, I didn't run. Not then. How could it end like that? Where's your sense of completeness? In this story I'm the fat lady, and I haven't sung yet."

"Well, get on with it then. I haven't got all night. And nor, I think, do you."

"Where did we get up to?"

"The police are stomping down the aisle."

"Oh, yeah."

The police marched towards the stage. I was running out of time. I ignored Vole and appealed directly to the Shank.

"Mr Shankley," I said, my voice sounding strained and breathless and slightly crazy even in my own ears. "Please just give me five minutes to explain. I've figured out what's going on. The whole thing. All of it."

"Ignore him," said Vole mildly. "There is a medical history. The boy is deranged. He is ill. And, as I said, dangerous."

The Shank stared at Vole and then at me. Whatever the true nature of the power relations between them, in public he usually deferred to the Principal. I didn't know which way this was going to go.

"Let the boy speak," he said, after what felt like hours, but must only have been a couple of heartbeats. Then he turned to me, his eyes burning. "Two minutes. Then you're finished."

I nodded. Two minutes would do. I took a breath.

"Let me tell you a tale. It's the story of a bitter and frustrated man. A man devious enough to hide his true nature behind a kindly and bumbling exterior. A man bent on … *revenge.*"

I paused and looked around the audience. I had them. They were silent. They were listening.

"My mistake," I continued, "was to think it was you, Mr Shankley. I thought that you wanted to destroy the Drama Queens because they represented everything that you despised. They were the spirit of misrule, of carnival, when you wanted order and discipline. You just needed an excuse to close them down. So I assumed that you'd sent your henchmen, Bosola and Funt, to do the dirty work, murdering the stick insects and then the rest of the animals.

"But then a mistake was made. The guinea pigs ended up in the wrong locker…" I cast a quick glance at Zofia, who looked back at me without emotion. "The *right* locker wasn't mine, as I initially suspected. The bodies were supposed to be found in the locker of Emma West – our very own Dorothy."

I gestured extravagantly towards Emma. There were gasps from the audience, and from some of the others on the stage, but she only raised an eyebrow, and curved her wide mouth into the slightest of smiles.

"And I know exactly who it was who planted them there. It was the same person who killed the stick insects and the chickens, leaving fatal clues each time.

The first clue was the chopsticks thrown into the bin in the toilets. It took me a while to get my head round that. Then I came across someone who was so scared of bugs he'd go so far as to use a pair of chopsticks to avoid having to handle them directly. Someone who also had the opportunity to steal the chopsticks from their rightful owner."

I looked at Ling Mei. I tried to squeeze into that look some of what I was feeling. The regret, the sadness, the love. The lost possibility of a shared life and a peaceful old age. Probably too much to expect from a glance that lasted three quarters of a second.

"It was the same person who cut a hole in the chicken wire, knowing that a fox would take care of the rest for him. But he got careless. He dropped a feather in the cage – a feather from a boa. A boa worn by one of the Drama Queens. But not any old Drama Queen. This was a Queen who was prepared to betray his leader and everything he stood for in order to get the chance to become Dorothy. A kid who is right now up there, behind you all."

I pointed up to the control box, where Hart was manning (and I use the term loosely) the spotlight – the spotlight that had so perfectly picked out the tortoise. A thousand heads spun his way. I heard the word "traitor" coming from the luscious lips of Emma West.

But I hadn't finished, and the heads in the audience spun back to me as I carried on.

"Yes, Hart was the killer. But when a throat is slit, we don't blame the knife, do we? We blame the hand that holds the knife. So, Hart, come on down and join your boss, the real killer, our Principal, Mr Vole."

Now I had to shout over the commotion in the hall.

"Yes, you, Mr Vole; it was always you. Our friendly, bumbling, absent-minded, senile Principal. Fake, all of it. You loathed the New Regime, loathed losing your power. You would do anything, use anyone you could, to discredit and destroy the Shank. You used Hart and turned the Queens into pawns. And you murdered those animals. You didn't care who or what suffered as long as you could extract your revenge. You knew that if you could get the Shank to ban the play then he'd be the most hated figure in the history of the school."

There was a tense silence in the hall. It was broken by a low, sad, soft chuckle. A chuckle that seemed both sympathetic and mocking. A chuckle that put an arm around you so that it could more easily hold you up to ridicule.

"My boy, my poor boy." Vole sighed. "Nobody could think that I would dream of hurting any animal, least of all my old friend, the beloved Bede." He shook his head, slowly, sadly. "I blame myself. I should have seen this coming, given your history of mental illness. But I've always believed in giving a child the chance for redemption. Alas, on this occasion, it was a mistake… I left you in charge of the tortoise in my office. Miss Bickersniff will gladly confirm that, I am sure."

He looked over the top of his half-moon glasses at Miss Bickersniff – she nodded back. Of course she would. She didn't know what I knew.

And suddenly I saw the genius of the man. Like all great conspirators, he had a plan B. Plan A was to frame the Drama Queens, forcing Shankley to ban the play, with the added humiliation of the tortoise's big entrance. He'd be despised, a figure both of loathing and fun. Plan B, only to be used if Plan A was rumbled, was to set me up. It was a safety net that he had kept all along, ever since the moment he knew I'd been in that cubicle when Hart dumped the insects. I'd take the heat and he could carry on bumbling until he took his pension, or he thought up a new plan to get rid of the Shank. That was why he'd given me the key. Everything else that had happened to me – Big Donna's hit, the faked video footage in the Underworld – was intended to make me look like a psycho.

And it would have worked, it really would, if I hadn't seen that receipt.

But I *had* seen it, and now I spoke:

"Mr Vole, I know you wouldn't hurt the Venerable Bede. Stick insects, chickens, guinea pigs, yes. You felt nothing more for them than you did for the butterflies you asphyxiated. But you needed a last great gesture. It had to appear as though the school mascot had been slaughtered—"

"Appear? I can assure you, young man, that the tortoise is dead."

There was a titter of nervous laughter from the audience.

"*That* tortoise is dead. But *that* tortoise is not *our* tortoise."

"What on earth are you blathering about, boy?"

That was the Shank. My time and his patience were running out.

I took the slip of paper from my pocket. "This receipt is from a pet shop in town. I found it in Mr Vole's desk. On it is written, '1 t. cadaver, £4.' The manager of the pet shop told me that the 't' is for tortoise. 'Cadaver' means 'dead body'."

The crowd erupted into excited chatter. The Shank quelled it with a glare.

"Yes, Mr Vole, you bought a dead tortoise. A tortoise cadaver. The pet shop guy told me that two or three tortoises die there of natural causes every week. You snipped off the head with your bonsai shears, and planted the body here on stage. You slipped the real Bede into your pocket when your back was towards me in your office. Then you stashed him in your briefcase."

"Absurd, absurd." Vole laughed, but I could see the sweat beading like mercury on his forehead. It was time for my final gambit. Everything rested on this.

"Really? Well, then, would you please open up your briefcase."

I pointed to the old leather attaché case, which was propped beside the Principal's chair.

Suddenly the whole hall was one vast eye, focused on the Principal. His mouth opened, but no sound emerged. He gasped, guppy-like for breath.

I *pwned* him.

CHAPTER THIRTY-THREE
The Knife That Wasn't

"BRAVO, bravo," purred the cat. "You really said all that?"

"Well, you know, sorta, yeah. Mostly."

And in my mind that was how the scene had played out, and those were the words I had used. But who is to say exactly what is the truth? Remember your first day at junior school? Remember how big everything seemed? And by the time you were leaving, how that school seemed so small. And which view was the right one?

"I am impressed. Did Vole open the case or did he flee, his tail between his legs?"

"I'm getting to it."

I had triumphed. Vole wavered. The Shank glowered.

The crowd hung expectant, like the guillotine blade waiting to drop. Emma, Ling Mei, Zofia, they were watching me now, each with a new respect. It was the great moment. The moment I had been waiting for all my life. The point of singularity that initiates the Big Bang and presages the creation of everything.

And then came not the big bang, but a small crash, as the back door again burst open. A thousand faces turned.

Ms Cassandra was silhouetted in the doorway, her hair a mess, her clothing in disarray, a look of horror on her face.

"Beware, beware!" she shrieked. "He's got a knife!"

"*Beware*?" said the cat on the roof. "Who the hell says 'beware'?"

"You don't need to tell me. That alone should have alerted the crowd to the fact that she was a loony toon."

But it didn't. Her shrieks were answered by others.

I strode to the front of the stage.

"It's not a knife," I began. As I spoke I reached into my pocket with the intention of showing it to be empty. "It's a scalpel, and it's a meta—" But the "phor" got totally lost in the shouts and screams. The people on the stage fled from me. Even the kids in the audience surged back, falling over each other in their attempts to escape from me and my mythical blade. Ling Mei,

Dorothy, Mrs Maurice, all of them seemed to dissolve into the chaos, as if they'd never existed.

I looked around into a grinning face. The years had fallen from Mr Vole. He appeared young again and vigorous, and began to move towards me. I could see the headlines: *Courageous Principal Disarms Insane Schoolboy.*

In front of me, the police had woken from their slumber and were coming.

For a second I considered my options. I could stay and argue, but I knew that they would not let me speak, and that Vole would hide the briefcase or somehow spirit away the Venerable Bede.

There was a crunch and a stumble. Vole staggered. He'd stepped on the headless tortoise. I took my chance. I ran past him, stooped and grabbed his briefcase, and sped through the back of the stage like a phantom.

CHAPTER THIRTY-FOUR
SCHRÖDINGER'S TORTOISE

"AND this is it?" The cat nuzzled curiously at Vole's attaché case.

"Yeah, this is the case," I replied, my mind drifting away over the roofs.

"Have you opened it yet?"

"Hmmm? No, not yet."

"Why the hell not?"

"It's not that simple."

"Why?"

"Well, there are a couple of possibilities."

"Go on."

"OK. I open the case. There's a tortoise in there. I'm right. Vole's a psychopath."

"Or…"

"I open the case…"

"Yeah?"

"And there's nothing inside but some papers and a thermos flask of tepid soup."

"And what would that mean?"

"You know."

"Tell me."

"It would mean… It would mean that I'm … that I'm not seeing things the way they are."

"Your medication?"

"Yep, my medication."

"I see."

The cat went and peered over the edge of the roof, and then came back to my lap.

"They're waiting for you, you know."

"I know. I can see them."

"You must go down."

"Why?"

"You can't stay here for ever."

"I know."

"Then open the case."

"I don't want to go back to the hospital. I've had enough of the lies, and the drugs they give you to make you believe the lies, and the other drugs they give you because the drugs they give you to make you believe the lies make you sick."

I stood up, still cradling the cat, and moved to the edge. I wobbled a bit, and a sort of sigh came from the crowd. The particles that made up Ling Mei, Zofia and the others had re-formed down there. They were mixed up among the police and ambulance men, and the curious neighbours, and a man with a camera. My mum and dad and sister were probably down there, somewhere, but I didn't want to seek their faces.

"Don't hurt me."

"Of course I won't hurt you, Cat."

"But … you hurt the others. I mean you *might* have hurt the others."

"Which others?"

"The little ones."

"The little whats?"

"You know very well."

"Me, I don't know jack shit."

"The animals."

"You don't know what you're saying."

"But it's possible…"

"Whose side are you on?"

"Cats don't take sides."

"All that's necessary for the triumph of evil is for good cats to do nothing."

"Will you put me down, please?"

"I promise you, you're quite safe."

"You're not going to jump, are you?"

"Of course not. I don't want to die. I love life. Every day is a new adventure. And there are mysteries."

"Then what are you going to do?"

"I'm going to fly."

"Please don't. Open the case. Please open the case and see."

"It's fine. You're safe. We're together. Flying is easy, when you know how."

I stepped from the roof and though, for a second, I felt that I was indeed falling, soon the air caught under my wings and I began to soar. I soared over the crowd, their faces upturned and filled with rapture, because they were seeing the most beautiful thing. And then I was beyond the people and above the roofs, and I felt the starlight fall on my wings like warm snow, and I brought the cat to my face and breathed into the fur at the nape of her neck and

CHAPTER THIRTY-FIVE
The Last Chapter

"YOU oscillate its tit a lot."

"What?" I looked down. My feet were still on the hard edge of the world. I was cold. I didn't feel cold, but I must have been, because I was shivering.

"You oscillate its tit a lot."

"*What...?*"

"You oscillate its tit a lot."

"Don't just keep on saying that. What are you talking about?"

"It's the answer to the question."

"Which question?"

"How do you titillate an ocelot? Remember? Back at the beginning, on the toilet wall? You oscillate its tit a lot. It's a sort of spoonerism, I suppose."

"Oh, yeah, I see."

My toes were sticking out over the edge. I wiggled them. I'd been meaning to do something, but now I couldn't quite remember what it was.

"Just a simple play on words."

The cat was looking up at me. The look on her face was, I guess you'd have to say, one of cunning.

"Yeah, sure."

Something was troubling me. The cat. Those words.

"Hang on … how do you know what's written on the wall of a toilet cubicle in my school? When have you ever been to my school?"

"Oh, well, I'm not sure. I just know."

And then the cat said something else, but I couldn't really understand it. It was a sort of mewling. A cat noise.

"John."

The voice was behind me. I turned round. My dad was on the roof. He wasn't supposed to be here.

"What?"

"Why don't you come in, son? Mum and Cathy are waiting. They're worried. It's dangerous here, you might fall."

My dad stretched out his hand to me. I put the cat down. I took my father's hand.

ACKNOWLEDGEMENTS

UNLIKE most of my books, *Hello Darkness* had a prolonged and agonizing birth. That it saw the light of day is down to the encouragement – and criticism! – of my agent, Philippa Milnes Smith, my friends Noga Applebaum and Tanya Epstein, and my editor at Walker, Annalie Grainger. Each helped to shape the final narrative, taking something that began as insane and unreadable and turning it into something a little less insane and, I trust, much more readable. So, my profound thanks to them.

ANTHONY McGOWAN's novels for young adult readers include *Hellbent* and *Henry Tumour*, which won the Booktrust Teenage Prize and the Catalyst Award. *The Knife That Killed Me* was shortlisted for the Booktrust Teenage Prize and longlisted for the Guardian Children's Fiction Prize. It is to be released as a movie in autumn 2013. Anthony was born in Manchester, brought up in and around Leeds and lives in London.

DAYLIGHT SAVING

When Daniel Lever accompanies his dad to the Leisure
World Holiday Complex, his expectations are low. But then
he sees a mysterious girl by the fake lake and everything
changes. Lexi is funny and smart, but why does she have
wounds that get worse each time they meet? And is her
watch really going backwards?

As the end of British Summer Time approaches, Daniel has
to act quickly. Their souls depend on it.

**"Ed's voice is utterly distinctive: strong, emotive,
haunting."** *Hilary Mantel*

Everything you know is wrong.

THE TRUTH IS DEAD

Everything you know is wrong…

New truths from eight award-winning authors:
Philip Ardagh
Frank Cottrell Boyce
Anthony McGowan
Linda Newbery
Mal Peet
Marcus Sedgwick
Eleanor Updale
Matt Whyman